VOICES
IN THE
CEDARS

PATRICIA EKKER HOLDEN

ISBN 979-8-89112-183-6 (Paperback)
ISBN 979-8-89112-184-3 (Digital)

Covenant Books
11661 Hwy 707
Murrells Inlet, SC 29576
www.covenantbooks.com

Dedicated to my father, Richard Ekker, rancher in Utah's West Desert Sheeprock Mountains, where antelope dance with coyotes across the hardpans of the desert beneath rain clouds of purple and pink, racing to color far blue mountains in wine hues. Dust devils whirl through shad scale and fall upon the foothills, where wildflowers and sagebrush nod in rhythm to the wind. Further up in the canyons, Hereford cattle graze in comfort while rain gives new life to the grass and quakies along the ridges.

Dad was a World War I veteran, wounded in action, served with honor, and mustered out of the army in 1919 at Fort Douglas. Keeping a prayer in his heart that his family would be able in his absence to keep the ranch and cattle going, hoping he could live through the battles he fought across France and not shed his life's blood on foreign soil, being able to return home to the life he loved in Utah to parents who had renounced their Old Country for this new one: America, land of the free.

INTRODUCTION

Wild Sanctuary

Sunlight beams on pine bows, gently warming
dew dampened blades of meadow grass
Musty, earth, mountain aromas dance like stars in the night sky
White puffs of air float across an endless blue horizon,
blending in places between earth and space
Breezes stir aspen leaves, pushing branches, rippling
waters, moving air as if energy was exhaled from the
universe in awe of this pure, unspoiled place.

—R. Holden
March 13, 2021

CHAPTER 1

Staring the mule in the face, Wade slowly got the halter rope around its neck then took in the slack, carefully worked the halter over his long ears, and fastened the buckle. The mule stood complacently, quiet and calm. Wade decided this would be easier than he thought. Usually, when he walked into the corral, the mule's teeth would show with ears back, and wild-eyed head-on assault began. After a couple of rounds around the lone cedar tree in the center of the corral, only then could the twelve -year-old boy approach the twenty-three-year-old mule with any amount of daring. When he was told by his dad to get the mule caught, harnessed, and hooked to the wagon, Wade prepared for the daily battle. If his dad, Henry Emmerich, went to the corral to perform the same task, the mule responded like an old milk cow. Why the animal hated him so, he had no idea, but since it did hate him anyway, he decided his older brother's idea of hoisting the animal up on the beef gallows would be fun, entertaining, and payback time.

Leading old Buckums from the corral, Wade headed straight for the beef gallows, a huge frame built from four pine trunks with braces in each corner and an iron winch that his father used to pull a butchered beef or hog up to prepare it for preservation largely consisted of the beef gallows. It was nearly fourteen feet tall. Across the bottom forming a square were four huge poles that were attached to each other and the side poles with hand-forged metal strips. Henry and William, with Henry's brothers Bran and Jake, had driven two teams some miles west and up a canyon to where the pines grew tall and straight. There they had cut the needed poles and dragged them behind the wagons back to the ranch, where they built the gallows.

At times the boys rigged up swings and winched each other up as high as they dared, then swung across the top poles in daredevil fashion. They mostly did this when their fathers were out in the fields.

As Wade approached the gallows with the mule, brothers Dan and Ben were waiting for him. "Did Dad see you?" asked Dan.

"No, and I hope he's still up in the field," said Wade.

Big grins on their faces, they began wrapping the mule in the leather cradle and fastened it around his girth just behind his front legs. The idea was that when his front legs came off the ground, his hind legs would soon follow, and they could get him swinging.

After a few quick looks around, with no parent in sight and apparently on their own enough to warrant "the Plan" to be put into operation, Wade and his brothers began winching. As old Buckums began his unplanned rearing in the front end, he tried to get away, and too soon, his back end began heaving off the ground. He started kicking and struggling, which made the cradle slip back into his flanks. Down went his front feet to touch the ground, and up went his rear end. A perfect bucking horse flank strap couldn't perform any better. The old mule squealed a hoarse whinny and bucked, fought, kicked, and twisted.

About that time, Father came tearing out of the cabin, screaming, "What are you doing? You young fools will kill that mule!"

Then the beef gallus began trembling and swaying, and the yells of direction to put him down became yells of panic that the beef gallows would collapse and kill the mule and the boys! Eventually, old Buckums was restored to the good earth from his impromptu flying, and the gallows remained standing. Later in Wade's life, if his little daughters wanted to swing on the gallows, they were reminded it had been shook to its very foundations once and wouldn't stand for any more swinging.

Sitting his horse on the ridge above Alder Canyon, alone with his memories, Wade Emmerich watched the setting sun change gun metal gray rain clouds into shades of pink. Granite shoulders of the mountain pushed into the sky, mahogany and quake aspen growing along its collar, with oak and cedar flanking its foothills. Icy springs fed streams in every canyon, and his cattle grew fat on their summer range. Deer, elk, and other wild animals lived on his mountain while antelope and coyotes chased dust devils across the hardpans of the desert below.

Wade thought nowhere else could have such sunsets across the desert with rows of mountains in the distance and colors of pink, mauve, gray-black, and purple stretched across the horizon. Silver sage turned purple, and mountain tips rained gold and blue as the sun crept toward its rest beyond the hills. No place on earth brought him such contentment, such a sense of belonging, and the pull that this ranch placed on his heart and his childhood memories was enough to draw him back from no matter where he roamed.

Thinking of his childhood and rearing by parents determined to keep him on the right path brought tears to his eyes, dashed away with a quick hand. Tears in the eyes of a man seemed to make that man weak, Wade thought.

Knowing his aunt and uncles were living in the territory helped strengthen his resolve to keep his own brothers and sisters living well and being good people. His uncle Bran was a living example of what good people could become. Working hard to bring clean drinking water to the town of Indian Flats had brought people's thankfulness for removal of cholera in their midst with appreciation for Bran to an all-time high—most of them, anyway.

Wade thought of the Coombs, living down valley from Indian Flats, in a long, wide wash created from centuries of floods, which was named Coombs Wash. Half hillbilly, half white trash, never working an honest job, old Andrew Coombs had a half-starved wife and family of nine kids. He would whip his skinny mules into town, pulling a broken-down wagon, yelling at anyone who got near his wife or kids. After reaching a hitching pole, he would jump down and head for the nearest saloon. His wife would sit in the hot sun until he came back, never speaking or making eye contact with any-one. There was usually a bushy-haired, sunburned, and barefoot kid or two with her. He could be heard clear down the street shouting at her, "Git down, go git the dern flour, and hurry it up. Don't make me come lookin' fer ye!"

Wade knew, as well as everybody else, he had told her to wait in the wagon until he got himself a drink.

Old man Coombs hated Bran with an unnatural hatred. Bran had ridden past their run-down hangout one day to catch Coombs beating his wife hard about the shoulders and hitting her in the face, screaming obscenities as he hit her. Bran piled off his horse and upon reaching the crazed man, jerked him around and with one punch, knocked him clear across the yard and unconscious. Gathering Mrs. Coombs up, he carried her into her house and asked one of the kids who had been hiding behind whatever broken old furniture there was inside the house to show him where he could lay her down. The oldest boy pointed to the blanket hanging on the wall at the back of the house, and pushing it aside, Bran took her in and laid her on their bed. One of the kids came with a rag dipped in water, and Bran let her bathe her mother's face. After making sure she was breathing, he asked her if he could send the doctor out. She gasped, "No! Oh, no! He will kill me for sure. You can't stay here. Just leave. I will be all right."

Bran nodded and walked out to where the old man was trying to stand up. He grabbed his arm and helped him to his feet. When Coombs looked at Bran, he started to swear and told him, "I will kill you sure!"

Bran jerked his arm and twisted it up behind his back until he began blubbering. "Now, Coombs, I say just one thing. If I ever learn of you so much as touching your little wife in anger or just to torment her, I will come back here, and I will castrate you. Your kind shouldn't be allowed to marry or have children, but since you have, by the good Lord, you will hear me this day, and do you ever mistreat her or them, I will avenge them."

The old man's face whitened, and he dropped his head.

"Do you hear me?" Bran roared into the old man's face.

Coombs nodded.

"Okay, then, I will leave. Don't ever forget what I told you." Bran then climbed back on his horse, spurred him to a walk, and headed on down the wash. Total silence followed.

Ever since that encounter, no matter what Bran suggested or worked to get accomplished for the town, Coombs voted against it. Bran decided Coombs was just a thorn in his side, which would probably fester and aggravate until the narrow twisted old man either shriveled up and died or somebody killed him.

Although when forced into it Bran's temper exploded, Bran was usually even-tempered and fair with people. The territory was wild and not much law around, and people wanted him to run for sheriff. But Bran respected Sheriff Tom Hanks in Indian Flats and wouldn't consider running against him. He knew he could do much good by working with the water system and eventually working to improve the town by getting a church and a school built.

⸻ • ⸻

CHAPTER 2

Emigrants from Zwolle, Holland, in 1888, Wade's grandparents William and Catherine Emmerich never learned to speak English well. Honest and hardworking, William, born in 1845, and Catherine, born in 1849, wanted their children to emigrate to America, although not all had come with their parents, and it was doubtful those who stayed in Holland would ever leave their homeland. Their oldest son, Henry, had left Holland in 1881, traveling the continent of his newly adopted country to finally settle in a cupped valley full of wildflowers, sweet tall grass, and rushing icy streams among the Portage River mountains of Montana. Three of Henry's brothers—Jacob, Branlen, and Evert—decided to emigrate in 1883 and upon arrival in the wild Montana Territory wilderness, had settled in nearby canyons and foothills of the Portage River's drainage.

The joy shared between the brothers upon their reunion on the western edge of the American continent was a wonder. Much backslapping, laughter, and bear hugs were shared. "I thought you had come to the end of the earth, old son," declared Jake to Henry. "While we were trailing those wagons across those great plains, I thought you had lost yourself forever out here and we would never find you."

Laughing, Bran told Henry, "Yeah, Jake here decided the mules and oxen pulling the wagons were going too fast, so he chose to walk much of the way!"

Henry, looking at his younger brother incredulously, asked, "Really? You actually preferred to walk instead of ride?"

Jake, with a grin, said, "Yes, brother. I don't like speed, and them critters would get going awfully fast at times. I felt better trailing along beside them. And one day in the hot sun, I crawled on the back of one of the wagons and hung my feet over so I could jump if things sped up!"

Evert, the quiet brother, just stood by and grinned.

Jacob discovered a love for the tall mountains and prospecting. He loved the solitude, peace, and quiet. Solid ledges reflected sunlight, making them appear like molten silver running down the sides softening their barren hard surface, hoping daily to find a rich strike of gold or silver from which he would build a mine and make his fortune.

At this time, he had cut logs and built a cabin up in the canyon above Henry's place, where quaking aspen, pines, and scrub oak covered the draw, providing shelter and shade from sun and storms. A cold spring ran from under a nearby ledge, chuckling down the ravine into the main canyon, and Jacob knew he could have access to the water during every season. He preferred walking to any other mode of transportation, not enjoying the speed of a wagon or riding a horse. He loved the freedom of a long walk, going where his legs carried him, and seeing a new view over every mountaintop.

He was strong and healthy from the exercise and hard work. He did develop a slight stoop as he grew older, resulting from the shoveling and work on his tunnels. Jake bought shovels, picks, and a metal wheelbarrow for his mining activities. He could carry most of his tools easily into the steep-sided canyons, undergrowth choking the creek bottoms, and when he found the perfect outcropping of an ore possibility, he would set up camp and begin digging. Having a wagon and team would have been easier but not possible to get through the country he prospected. He often climbed high into the mountains and would begin a tunnel on the sidehill of a canyon.

In one such place, above the cabin he had established, he was digging into the mountainside and running a tunnel around a bend, following a showing of quartz with a few granules of gold embedded within it. As he worked, he noticed that the quartz seemed to be rotten, breaking apart easily from the thrust of the pick, and he could actually pick up small gold nuggets falling out of the veins in the quartz. His mind on this new event and wondering how he could best collect the gold without losing so much, he then noticed a dribble of sandy dirt running down the side the tunnel. His headlamp picked up the movement, and he straightened up and stared. Then in an instant, all hell broke loose as a rumble began deep within the mountain, and rocks began to slide.

He turned and ran with all his strength, when a rock slab came loose and hit his shoulder, knocking him into the wall of the tunnel. The slab traveled down his arm and smashed upon the upper part of his hip. Knocked off his feet, he still kicked and crawled and on hands and knees, crawled out the opening.

Falling against the dump outside, with his face lying in the dirt, he felt then heard more movement behind him. Rolling over, he saw the dirt belching out the tunnel mouth, and he felt it falling on him. He tried to stand but couldn't seem to get his legs under him, so he fell, crawled, and dragged himself off the dump and down the bank into the nearby creek. Lying there, it seemed that he was watching the devil himself blowing dark dirt and dust and even a few small rocks out the tunnel entrance.

He finally crept over to a quaken aspen and pulled himself to his feet. His hip felt like it was broken, but legs, arms, and ribs were okay; shoulder felt broken too. He wished with all his heart that day he had driven the team of mules up to the mine, but he had chosen to walk, as he usually did. So grabbing a forked stick, he broke it up to work as a single crutch. He worked up the bank and onto the narrow trail/road and began the painful walk down canyon.

After only a few feet, he couldn't bear the rubbing under his arm from the raw wood. He leaned against a tree and stripped his shirt off. He always wore long handles, so he didn't feel naked. He took his pocketknife out and cut the shirt in half then tied it around the makeshift crutch. That felt better. Then he found another stick and broke it to size and wrapped it in the other half of the shirt. Although his shoulder hurt terribly, he couldn't stand putting weight on his hip, so he used both sticks under each arm and swung the leg as he struggled down the canyon.

After a walk of a mile or more, he finally stumbled into his cabin. Shutting the door, he staggered to his bunk and slowly lowered himself upon it. Not removing shoes or clothes, he pulled the blankets up to his neck and closed his eyes.

CHAPTER 3

It was unusual for Jake not to visit the ranch and his parents every week, so when he didn't show up in three or four days, Henry saddled up his gray gelding Sam Boy and rode up to the cabin nestled in the aspens next to Spring Creek. He shouted out to his brother and got no answer.

Getting off the horse, Henry tied him to a nearby brush and walked to the door. Knocking once, he opened the door, and as his eyes adjusted to the dark inside of the cabin, he saw Jake on his bed. Jumping across the room, he grabbed Jake by the shoulders and yelled, "What's the matter? Jake, for God's sake, answer me!"

Jake moaned and said, "Don't scream so much, and don't take the name of Father God in vain!" Then he told Henry about the cave-in and his close call. Henry got him up to a chair and built the fire up, fixing coffee.

After they drank and as Jake was finished his coffee, Henry packed bedding in the wagon outside and caught Jake's team and harnessed them up then hooked them up to the wagon. He went back inside, got Jake on his good leg, and helped him out and into the wagon. Turning his own horse into the pasture where the mules had been, he climbed up onto the wagon seat, grabbed the reins, and clicked his tongue at the mules. Down they went to the main ranch.

After arriving there, Henry ran inside and told Mary about Jake. He asked where the kids were, and everyone was scattered about doing chores, some riding and others working on fences, so he ran up to his brother Branlen's cabin, praying he was around. He was sitting in the shade, working on a broken shovel. At Henry's arrival and by the look on his face, Bran knew something was terribly wrong. Henry told him in a hurry and asked that he come with him as he drove Jake to Indian Flats, where a doctor was. Bran ran with Henry back down to the yard where the wagon and team were with Jake in the wagon, jumped in, and headed out.

After several hours on the road, stopping on occasion to give Jake water and check on him, they made it to Indian Flats. The doctor checked him over and wanted him to stay in town for a few days so he could take care of him. Jake protested but was weakened by the long wait for Henry to find him and the long wagon ride to town. He went rather meekly for such a hardworking, strong, independent man.

After a few days, the doctor determined the shoulder and hip were not broken but badly bruised and scraped. Jake never walked straight again and always limped a little on the injured leg. His sister-in-law Mary was sure there was a bone chip inside the skin at the top of the hip, but she couldn't get it out unless she operated, and she wasn't a doctor. Jake said it was little enough to pay for his accident that easily could have taken his life.

When a wagon trail was established into a canyon by another miner or a developing mine, Jake brought a mule and a slide carrying a mine car and rail to set up in his new tunnel. This made his work easier getting ore out of the tunnel and onto the dump. But he gave up the cave-in within the tunnel near the canyon bottom, gold or no gold. He had several handfuls of nuggets in his pocket and kept them all the days of his life. He removed the window pane around the window in his cabin and there hid his nuggets, replacing the pane with screws instead of nails. He said once that was his retirement money.

CHAPTER 4

Bran found the small town of Indian Springs interesting with much opportunity for growth, although he lived in a cabin and was starting a ranch of his own with a small herd of cattle. He discovered a deep love for his new country with its wide-open spaces, freedom to choose what life he wanted, and intention to someday help with development and improvement within Indian Springs, which needed a school, a church, and refinement. He wanted to be a part of that.

Bran missed his twin sister Bronwyn, who had wanted to emigrate with him in 1883 but had been overruled by their parents, who insisted she stay and travel with them when they came. He missed her sense of adventure, laughter, and independence. She could always make him see fun and opportunity around them both. She was sixteen years old when he left with their brothers to find America and their new home. For days, Bran kept looking around the ship for her, thinking that with her determination and sense of adventure, she would stow away.

Evert became involved in helping develop reservoirs and irrigation systems upon the open range, where cattle and farming operations were starting up. His vision of the future included getting water to the many farms from the reservoirs through proper engineering. In Holland with water everywhere, his knowledge of its control through dikes and canals brought needed expertise to the western part of the undeveloped American continent.

Evert sent out word to surrounding ranchers and farmers that there would be a meeting held on Friday night. When the men gathered, he welcomed them. "As you know, we have been trying to figure ways to get the water out of the river and onto our land without it flooding and washing everything we have planted away. Last year, after we worked so hard to dig the new ditch down across the top of the valley floor and got water in it and actually onto our land, what happened? A cloud burst upstream, and here came a flood carrying trees, boulders and swept the ditch completely away, directed part of the floodwaters down onto the fields. And by the time it was done, all we had was another deep wash and debris all over the area we were trying to farm."

At this point, a man spoke up. "Yes, Evert, but how can we harness Mother Nature? It's impossible. I say we just let the water run in the natural channels, and we quit trying to force her hand." This followed with several other voices, all filled with despair.

"Boys, there is a way to handle this, I tell you. Where I come from, the Dutch harnessed the sea and claimed hundreds of acres of land from her—profitable land and useable land. I would suggest this for you to think about. Let us try to make dikes, high dikes, and trench behind them for the water to flow through. When we get enough dikes, no matter how hard the floods become, we can harness them and direct them away from our farmland. Dredges built from wooden beams cut to the exact width of the canals will help us clean them out every spring, and a mule on each side the canal with the dredge hooked by chain to tugs on the mule harness will work.

"Building up the dikes to as high as needed to withstand the force of the water will require more workers and mules to pull the dirt banks together. Any suggestions?"

After a pause, a man spoke up. He said, "Why don't we use the fort builders blueprint? They mixed straw and clay with water in a man-made pond then walked their oxen back and forth over it until it was crushed together and mixed well. Afterwards, they built bales of the stuff and stacked it together into a wall that, when hardened, protected them from Indian attacks."

"Well, that sounds good and all that," said another man, "but what happens if a lot of flooding hits it?"

Evert replied, "Boys, we all have good ideas and questions. Keep going with this and we should come up with some ways that will work. I can tell you right now that old fort downcountry on the bend of the Peace River is still standing and has been standing for near on a hundred years. I bet it will still be there in another hundred. And it's made of the same stuff. We could apply the same material to our dike walls, and they will divert the water without eroding like plain dirt would. Where is a good source of clay around here, and who has material in their fields to use in place of straw?"

At this, the men began serious talk of rebuilding their fields and beginning work on a series of dikes, with canals reinforced with rock to direct the water back onto fields parched for lack of water.

Before the meeting broke up, several leaders in the town approached Evert, thanking him and slapping him on the back for his enthusiasm and ideas. They asked him to spearhead the entire project and said they thought the banker would support each farmer with a loan to rebuild when presented with such an industrious plan. Evert said, "I will consider it, and now let's go home and get supper!"

One day shortly after this meeting, Evert was in town working in his office. He had a cabin out near his parents and was starting to clear land for some fields. He had built near the river that rumbled down through a nearby canyon, its headwaters high up in Raft Mountain south of the Emmerich holdings. Knowing the layout of the countryside, he deliberately claimed this area for a good place to get water diverted from the river onto land he could get cleared and start raising crops to sell. Having an office in town made him available to those involved with him getting water to the town in better quality than a muddy ditch.

CHAPTER 5

He heard a thump outside and stood to look. There was an Indian sitting on a horse, staring at Evert's cabin door. Opening the door, Evert walked outside and looked back at the man. Black eyes with a flinty stare, round chin, high cheekbones, and greasy hair pulled into a knot on the back of his head, he sat his horse like he was going to just sit there and look. He had an ragged old army hat pulled over his head, and he wore dirty faded jeans with an equally dirty worn shirt. Also, a pistol stuck in the waistband of his pants.

Evert didn't say a word, just staring back. Finally, the Indian man said, "Need water. Need seed."

Evert kept his silence and waited for a bit, then the Indian said, "Me Posey. Camp up there," pointing to the foothills some distance from town.

"You come?" Evert said. "What for?" and he pointed at himself then the Indian.

After a minute, Posey said, "You help me get water on ground. You help me get seed to put on ground."

Evert said, "Posey, I can look at water. I have no seed. I can have you talk to the man with seed and the man with a plow."

After thinking on that, Posey said, "You come look at water first."

Evert said, "I have to go get my horse." He went back inside, put some papers in the safe he'd been working on, and shut the door on his way back out. Walking down the boardwalk with the Indian riding beside on the road, he went to the stable where he kept his black gelding. Saddling up, he wondered where the Indian camp was and how they planned to get water.

Once in the saddle, he turned to the road and followed Posey out to the north. Then Posey turned west and off the road onto a faint trail. After traveling several miles, he turned again and headed south into the foothills.

Evert knew there was a good stream of water coming out of most of the canyons on the Raft Mountain range and hoped the camp was near one of them. Sure enough, rounding a hill and coming into the mouth of a canyon, he could see the Indian camp. They rode right on by it onto a fairly flat-topped ridge. Posey drew up and signaled to Evert that this is where he wanted the water.

To Evert's surprise, there were a lot of Indians of every age already working on pulling brush, chopping at trees, and dragging stumps off with ponies and a few ragged, thin mules. Evert could see a remarkable pile of rocks that had been removed and piled along the edge of the clearing. He glanced at Posey to see Posey watching him intently. He said, "Let's go see the water."

Across the side of the clearing they rode, and presently, there was the water, a rushing, gurgling stream going down out of the canyon onto the desert below, going nowhere. Evert dismounted, and so did Posey. Walking along the ridge, he could see a slight indention veering off toward the creek, one which, with work, could be used to bring a goodly share of that water into harness for use on the high ground.

Showing Posey, he asked him if he would be willing to dig where he told him and get a ditch going. "Yes. Water will go where I want. This is my farm and my tribe, and I will clear it, plant it, and water it. You have to help me get seed and plow."

"Now look, Posey, I am not getting the seed," said Evert, "or the plow. You are. You go back with me to town, and I will get the men who have the seed and the plow to talk to you. You will have to trade with them. The seed man will want game, any game: deer, elk. If you have cattle, some cows. Do not trade anything you need for your family or tribe. You can get hunters to get the wild game. The plow man will want hides, any hides, perhaps the hides of the game you trade to the seed man. It is up to you to trade for the things you want."

After standing quietly for a while, Posey turned to Evert and said; "You come. You eat. Then you go back, and I will come tomorrow, and you go with me to talk for seed and plow."

Evert could see no good way to refuse food, so he said, "Let's go eat."

Riding back to the tepee camp, Posey rode up to one tepee, jumped off his horse, and walked to the flap, opened it, and was inside and out in a matter of a minute. Holding up a hand for Evert to wait on his horse, Posey walked to another tepee and opened the flap and went inside.

As Evert sat there, a movement at the first tepee caught his eye. An incredibly heavy Indian squaw, about five feet and maybe four inches tall, stepped out. She held an unbelievably long sharp knife and stood and glared at Evert for a long moment, then she waddled around behind the tepee, and there suddenly was a gurgling bark and whine. After a minute or two, she came walking back, dragging a bleeding dead dog, which she immediately hung up onto a rack at the side of the tepee.

Evert felt his eyes would fall out. As she began gutting the animal, he kneed his horse toward the other tepee into which Posey had entered and not come out of. He yelled for him and then felt bile coming up in his throat. That the dog was going to be *lunch*, there was no doubt—hot, rare dog. No way was he going to stay and eat.

No answer. Was Posey having a nap? He yelled again and then kneed his horse to leave. The flap was thrown back, and out stepped Posey, a disgusted look on his face. "You getting hot, white man?"

"Yes, I am getting hot. I threw up out there and can't eat anything now. I have to leave and get home and take some medicine."

Posey looked behind Evert at the squaw skinning the dog, raised an eyebrow, and said, "Don't like dog, white man?"

Evert nearly choked. He had never seen an Indian raise an eyebrow before. He knew he had to get out of there before he really did throw up, and he mumbled, "See you in town tomorrow." Jerking the reins, he kicked his black's sides and loped out of camp. Once away from the camp, he began to laugh. Never in a hundred days would his brothers believe him when he told them his story.

Next morning, into the yard in front of Evert's office rode Posey. This time, he climbed down off his tired-looking horse and approached the door. Evert opened it and looked him in the face. "Want some coffee?"

Posey nodded, and Evert motioned him inside.

As they sat at the table with their coffee, Posey said, "You ready to talk to those men?"

Evert said he had talked to them, and they were interested in trading with Posey. However, Posey would have to do his own negotiation. Posey frowned then agreed. "But you come with me."

Evert said okay he would, and they walked down the street to the livery stable where the other men were waiting.

As they entered the building, Posey stared at the men until Evert introduced them all. "Posey, this is Earl Maxwell, and he has a plow he might be willing to loan you in trade for hides. You will talk about that. This here is Duncan Williams, who has some extra seed that would make good pasture. You will talk about trading with him for meat supplies: deer, elk, fish.

"Boys, this is Posey. Now, go ahead. I am going over here and sit on a crate while you do your trading."

A year later, in the area known as Indian Farm, there was a flat area on top of a long ridge. Water had been diverted from a wash in a draw nearby, up along the side of the ridge, until it ran freely onto the ridgetop. The Indians successfully harvested rangeland grass on that ridgetop. The Indian people living there and working the land were proud of their accomplishments, and some of the white farmers from down around Indian Flats had come up and seen what they had done. Some offered to help cut the grass for more trading. Posey proved shrewd and careful, and his family never went hungry. Evert and Posey became friends for the rest of their lives.

◆ ● ◆

CHAPTER 6

All four of William and Catherine's sons grew to love their new homeland and cherished the wide-open spaces with land to work, ranches to establish, and freedom from Holland's oppressive restrictions. Too many people in small places, restricted by government control and with high taxes and low wages, propelled the Emmerichs into poverty. Limited education forced dependence on more than one job. School was affordable by only the upper class. School was for the upper class, and common people weren't supposed to dream of an education. Away from the stifling mother country facing challenges never before heard of—with sweet, clean air and water; grass up to their horses' chests; and the allowance by a young country to begin a new life and own their own land—the boys felt they were in heaven.

On the day the brothers reunited in Montana Territory in the foothills of the Raft Mountain range, the three new arrivals sized up their older brother Henry. Henry had been working hard and had a long cabin built of newly cut and barked cedar logs, with long pine logs across the top as ridgepoles. He cut isinglass crystals to fit into openings he had made in the walls for windows. Cloudy and somewhat distorted, the crystal sheets worked for letting light into an otherwise dark interior. Wearing canvas trousers and a faded work shirt, Henry looked as tough as the land he walked in. Long dark hair topped with a ragged leather hat shadowed his eyes. Henry had high cheek bones and broad shoulders, with calloused and scarred hands. As the brothers carefully watched their elder brother, they saw a patriot to this new country and listened to his words and dreams of a new future in it. They learned of his ranch and began to catch a glimmer of the man he had become since leaving Holland.

The boys held regular meetings to discuss their plans and keep track of each other and learn any news they may have heard from their parents. They'd all written letters, encouraging their parents to emigrate. The letters promised opportunities in Montana Territory to build a wonderful life and stay in close contact with each other.

━━━━━━━ ▪●▬ ━━━━━━━

CHAPTER 7

While the boys were deciding where they would take up land and begin their own cabins and corrals and clear their own land, they stayed with Henry. Talking into the night, laughter filled the air, and nothing felt more right. They spent many hours, sometimes days, in the surrounding wilderness, learning the lay of the land and making decisions as to where they wanted to sink roots. Sometimes they camped out, and they eventually settled on areas their hearts and spirits were spoken to by the beautiful, wild wide land, and open skies.

Only Bronwyn was coming with her parents, and leaving the rest of their family in the mother country while they left for new uncharted frontiers was heart-wrenching and terrifying. She knew her mother, Catherine, spent hours on the ship crying for those of her children, grown now, with families of their own, knowing she very likely would never see them again. But times were desperate in Holland, with few jobs to be found and famine hovering over the land.

Catherine knew if she and her husband didn't leave now, they never would. Selling their small business before they lost it and home and whatever belongings they didn't need, they barely had enough for passage on the ship and food until they landed in America. Parting was also difficult for Bronwyn. She realized they had no future in Holland, but to leave her sister and a brother, who were both married and had small children, was almost unbearable. To think they would probably never see them again broke her heart.

In spite of the parting, Bronwyn couldn't wait to begin her journey to a new life in America. She couldn't wait to see her twin brother Branlen again. His letters reminded her that she could become any-

20

thing she wished and would find love in that free open country, with choices to make that only she could make, with no one forcing her or limiting her options. Now twenty-three years old, she felt she could make her dreams come true. Even religion was her choice to choose in America, with no restrictions placed on her like Holland had. The mother church in Holland was one run by the government, and everyone had to belong to it, or they were ostracized from their very homes and villages, some to living as beggars or worse in order to survive.

As Bronwyn held the railing of the ship and watched the waves rolling beneath the huge keel of the ship, her reminiscences led her back to her brother Bran. He had offered to help finance her in an endeavor she had written him about with her purchasing a building in town and opening a shop for ladies' wear, everything from undergarments to dainty hats, with hand and face lotions in between.

Bronwyn knew she could do this and with energy, work, and determination, envisioned a business strong enough to withstand frontier trials. Getting the attention of the hardworking women would be the challenge because she was sure they would consider such things as frivolous and not worthy of sacrifice to get them. However, Bronwyn decided that she would teach them how to use the hand lotions and face creams to prevent their skins from drying out in the sun and wind as they went about their chores. One step at a time, and then it would be like the need to place curtains at the windows of a shanty and a tablecloth on the table, something to soften the harshness of the land. From there, it would be proven that delicate undergarments, instead of the plain cotton and canvas that chafed tender skin, could be worn on special occasions. Even a stylish hat instead of the usual sunbonnet could be worn on occasions. Yes, she would provide these things for her fellow settler sisters, and she would do it to help bring them grace, dignity, and better self-worth.

Knowing she had to have an outlet for the things she would have to purchase, Bronwyn walked back to her little stateroom and sat down on her bed. Drawing a sheet of precious paper from her trunk, she began listing all the possibilities, including a lady to weave straw hats. If she could possibly hire some help, that would be a plus, but for the moment, she would have to make the soap, lotions, and creams herself, and as she saved enough money to purchase other necessities, she could go on from there. She wouldn't be a burden to her family, and she hoped she could even, in time, help her parents financially.

Bronwyn also knew she wanted a future with freedom to go and do and eventually own a horse, learn to ride, and travel beyond the farthest hills just for the pure joy of it. She wanted her own cabin, and she wanted independence. Yet she also felt the draw in her heart for a companion to walk beside her through life and to bring into this new world new souls whom she could teach to worship Father God and to love this new land and to contribute to in better ways. Yes, Bronwyn had her dreams, and she held them close deep within.

Standing on shore at Vollenhove, near the docks where the huge ship with sails unfurled was waiting for passengers, Catherine felt as though she was stepping off the very earth. She and William had left Bronwyn sitting by their trunks while they, ready to sign rosters, visited the offices. Filling in paperwork for departure to America took several hours, along with the money it took to pay for passage on the ship. The finality of their decision to leave the old country for the new took their breath away. Signed documents to be filed in archives were handed to the proper authorities. Walking back to the dock where Bronwyn waited, they watched while sailors worked and shouted as they completed unfurling the giant sails on their waiting ship.

━━━●━━

CHAPTER 8

Once aboard the massive ship, moving out of Dutch waters and into the blue waters of the ocean, Catherine and William knew there would be no changing their minds. Oddly enough, this brought them both a final sense of relief.

Bronwyn felt the ocean beneath the ship as the waves took it into their grasp once cleared from shore. She couldn't sit in the hold, where the bunks were, and raced up the steps to the deck, where she watched the ocean and the white waves along the ship as it plowed along on its course toward America. No longer able to see land anywhere, her excitement heightened as she sensed this was a trip into a new life, a new beginning, and she was up to the challenge. She would make a name for herself and her family when she reached the land where Bran had settled, and she would never again look behind her.

Shrugging away the thought that perhaps she would become an old maid since she was twenty-three years old now, she decided to seek her future come what may and give the Western world a stir with her own stamp upon it. Back to her earlier musings, she knew she could provide fine linens, personal items, handmade soaps and lotions, potions of fragrance and books, bringing a touch of civilization from East to West.

Catherine met and became friends with a frail, sickly woman who, although she fought health problems, hand sewed lovely kerchiefs and linens. One day, Eenie told Catherine, "I wonder if I will make it to America? I feel so dizzy and miserable. I don't think this passage will find me with it at the end."

Catherine, alarmed, replied, "Oh, Eenie, you will soon get better, and we will walk together with our husbands across the drawbridge. You keep thinking about how you will raise your children there. It will be so much better than what we left behind."

Eenie smiled, and resting her head against the side of the berth, she said, "Caro, thank you for being my friend. You are about the only person aboard, besides my dear Elmer, who knows me and talks to me."

Weeks later, as the ship finally neared American shores and she could see land and the Statue of Liberty, Catherine felt faint with relief. Her strong husband stood by her side and spoke in a low voice, "There is our future, Caro my dear, and the future of our family. With God's will and strong backs, we will build lives for ourselves when we are reunited with the boys out west. They know we are coming if they received our letter, and now I have to find work to purchase tickets on a train west across the plains."

His words were spoken with determination and courage, yet Catherine still felt uncertain. Wondering about Bronwyn and her reaction to the ship and her enthusiasm during the crossing, she prayed silently that she would heed their warnings of caution with unknown people.

Thinking of her sons, who had emigrated years before, gave her strength, and reuniting with them would be sweet. She couldn't wait to meet Henry's wife. He had written that he had met a lovely young woman, born on the continent, living in Indian Flats. After a short courtship, they had married and were now expecting their first child. Caro prayed she would get to them before Mary gave birth. She would love to be the grandmother who welcomed the new little life into the world.

In the melee of people readying belongings on the deck and getting in lines to walk down the bridge onto Ellis Island, Catherine couldn't see Eenie and her family. When they disembarked from the ship, they walked unsteadily on sea legs not yet used to land into Ellis Island's government inspection post. Determining all new emigrants had sufficient means to support themselves on American soil, carried no infectious diseases, and were healthy mentally as well as physically was no quick task, and some were kept waiting seven hours. Luckily Catherine, William, and Bronwyn were declared approved in less time than that and given the go-ahead to proceed into the city of New York.

Running back into the fence dividing the inspected from those quarantined, she stared desperately to see Eenie. Suddenly, there was Eenie's husband and two children. "Elmer, where is Eenie? Elmer looked over at her and wearily shook his head. Motioning behind him, he came to the fence and said, "They are holding her in quarantine because she is so weak, and they think she is contagious. What with they have no idea, but she will not be allowed to continue on."

Caroline began to shake. "How long?"

Elmer replied, "Maybe two weeks, maybe two months. I don't know, and I don't know if she can live through this. They said I could leave her here and take the children and go if only to find a shelter and work, but that would kill her for sure! Although, there are a few who are leaving their loved ones here to heal alone. For your children's sake, take care of yourself, Caroline, and pray for us."

"Oh, Elmer, please promise me you will write and let us know where you are when she is well and you come onto the continent. Send to Indian Flats in Montana Territory. We will eventually get it. She is my friend, and I will pray for you both."

Unable to do anything else, Caroline made her way back to William put her arms around him, hugging him tightly, then grasping both Bronwyn's and her husband's hands, let him lead them onto the small strip of land going onto America's east coast.

✦

CHAPTER 9

After inquiring of people on the street, William led his weary wife into a small boardinghouse, where he left her to rest. Bronwyn begged to go with him, but he refused, telling her, "You have to stay with your mother until I find out if there is any work out there and get the feel of the people and the area where we are. It might be dangerous for a young woman in this area. Stay here!" He immediately headed out to check on possible work.

Searching through neighborhoods, storefronts, and even bars, William was fortunate to discover a blacksmith shop. Walking in, he spoke to the man bent over an anvil, pounding on a mule shoe. The man straightened his back slowly and turned and looked at William. "What can I do for you?" he asked.

William replied in Dutch, "I have worked as a blacksmith at home"

"Stop," said the man. "I can't understand you. What do you want from me?"

At that, William walked over and picking up blacksmith tongs, grabbed a small piece of metal, thrust it into the hot forge coals, and after it turned red with the heat, took it to the anvil and expertly hammered it into a perfect half oxshoe. Holding it up for inspection, he then dipped it into a tub of water nearby to temper the metal so it wouldn't be brittle. The man held out his hand and said, "You are hired." So William, working through hand signals and listening closely for familiar words, began to work for a fine man who patiently helped him with English words during his time there.

Eventually, William earned enough to pay their passage on a train across the continent. Bronwyn's excitement was contagious, and Catherine's enthusiasm grew more every day for the coming trip.

Finding passage on a train going as far west as Kansas was done. From there, they had to find a wagon train heading farther west into the territories.

Getting a couple of mules, harness, and wagon wasn't cheap, and William argued strongly for the lowest prices he could get. This was doubly difficult with his strong accent and lack of good knowledge of English. The very day they arrived in Salt Lake City, the three of them paid a visit to the post office, where they found a letter waiting for them from Bran. Instructions where a good team and strong wagon was waiting for them, paid for by William's sons, were within the letter. This was huge. William knew he would have had to work for a year to pay for the team and wagon. He mentioned to several men he met around the town that his worn-out mules and wagon were for sale, and though they sold cheaply, he still got a few dollars for them. Tears of joy filled William's eyes at the thoughtfulness of his sons, and he gently wiped them away.

William and Catherine walked to the livery stable, with Bronwyn following a short distance behind, looking in the storefront doors and through the windows. A wiry small man with an unkempt long beard met them. When William handed him the letter from Bran, he yelled, "I don't want you here waving foreign words at me! I can't read that jumble of junk! I don't know what you think you're playing at, but get the hell out of here before I call the law!"

William couldn't understand the words but understood the body stance. Snatching the letter from the old man's hand, taking Catherine's arm, and motioning to Bronwyn, he walked directly to the sheriff's office away down main street. "Sheriff, I need help," said William and at the same time holding up the letter. The sheriff, Dawson Cramer, couldn't read Dutch but knew someone who could. Meanwhile, handing a cup of coffee to her, the sheriff had Catherine wait inside the office on a chair placed by the table. Bronwyn refused to stay and insisted on accompanying him and the sheriff.

Motioning William to follow him, he headed up the street to a long, low building that housed a bar. William told Bronwyn she had to wait outside on the boardwalk until they were through inside. She leaned against the wall and watched the various people, yet looking at the tall Sheriff Cramer made her heart do funny things. He had shaggy brown hair and brown eyes that glittered with intelligence. His hands were shaped for work and were strong hands, beautiful hands. She felt her face grow hot with her thoughts and watched him while he listened to her father try to explain the situation with the livery man. While she idled beside the building, she wondered if he would help them or not.

Walking inside, the two men approached the man behind the bar. Speaking to the barkeep, the sheriff handed him the letter. After reading it, the man looked at William and shook his head. William's heart fell as he wondered if his son's money spent for the team and wagon had been stolen. The sheriff grinned when the barkeep told him what the letter said. Smiling at William, he said to come with him again. Outside, they collected Bronwyn, and motioning to him to follow when William stood there, he headed down the street to the livery.

As the sheriff walked in the door of the stable and the old man looked up and saw William with him, his face fell. "I can't help what that foreigner feller told you, sheriff, but he is lying!"

"This letter says pretty clear there is a paid-for team and wagon left here for you to take care of for these people. They've crossed an ocean and the country to get here, and you will provide the team and wagon as you were paid in full months ago as well as for the feed for the team of mules. So shut up, go get the team, harness them, and hitch them to the wagon. Have the rig out front in one hour. When we come back, be ready—unless, of course, you want to argue, and try cheating this man out of his family's money, like you've tried in the past!"

The sheriff looked calmly at the man, but something in his eyes made the little man squirm. Working his jaw, he dropped his head and muttering under his breath, headed for the back door to the corral. Not understanding many of the words but getting the gist of the sheriff's statements, William held out his hand. The sheriff shook his hand and said, "Good luck."

Through all of this, Bronwyn had watched carefully the sheriff's face, deciding he was a very fine-looking man with an angular jaw bone and dark handlebar mustache. His broad-brimmed hat was worn straight on his head, pulled down a little in front. A glint of humor was in his eyes yet a toughness that earned him respect. And when his eyes met hers, she saw something in them that showed more than a little interest. She smiled slightly, nodded her thanks to him, and quietly followed her father outside, quietly hoping that she would someday see this fine man again.

Walking back up the street, William went to the sheriff's office, collected Catherine, and with his limited English and the sheriff's help, found a tented building where good, simple food was served at a reasonable price. Bronwyn couldn't stop talking, telling her mother every move they had made and what the sheriff looked like. Her father watched her, eyebrows raised in consternation that she was impressed by the sheriff.

CHAPTER 10

After a hot meal and coffee, they finally headed for the livery. Upon arrival there, a team of mules were waiting with a used wagon hitched to them. William went inside where the glaring livery stable owner was sitting on an overturned barrel. He held out the letter and motioned sign language, insisting the old codger sign his name. After an X was placed at the bottom of the letter, William went out, helped Catherine into the seat, and after Bronwyn had clambered up on her own and settled on a small trunk in the back of the wagon, he gathered the reins, heading the team up the street to the north on the final leg of their long journey.

Catherine placed her hand upon William's arm, and as he glanced at her, she spoke. "Will, we need supplies for the trip and don't know how long it will take us. Let's stop at that big tent and see if they sell beans and flour."

Will, agreeing with his wife, turned the team into a clear area beneath a huge cottonwood tree. Jumping down, he asked Catherine, "Do you want to come with me? You won't get another chance for a long time to buy things, and maybe once inside, you'll see something you'll need."

She said yes, and after being helped down from the high wagon seat, she walked swiftly into the tented area. Finding flour, beans, coffee, some sewing needles, and a bolt of sturdy fabric, she sighed with relief and turned it all over to Will for purchase.

Bronwyn, having climbed quickly from the wagon almost before her dad had stopped it and set the brake, had different ideas as to what necessities were needed. She gathered more bolts of fabric for linens, dresses, and trim, followed with sewing supplies, and then she searched through the big tent for paper and inkwells. After finally finding several sheaves of paper, inkwell, and a packet of quills, she then looked for soap and lotion. Finding what she wanted, she then gathered several lengths of brightly colored ribbons and lace for hats and dress trim.

William had had enough waiting on his daughter's shopping and motioned to her to gather her purchases to the counter, where he carefully counted out money to pay for all of it. He frowned at her purchases and said, "Bronwyn, we can make soap and lotion, and you will have to settle for that!"

She stared at her father and with a determined tilt to her chin, replied, "Dad, I have to have these things. I can't make them without an example for ingredients and scent. I only want one bottle of each, and I can make almost exactly the same thing once we get established and I get the ingredients for them."

With a disgusted sigh and shrug, Will paid for Bronwyn's purchases and handing them to her, motioned to the door.

CHAPTER 11

Back at Ellis Island, Elmer had a visit with his wife, Eenie. They talked quietly for some time, then Eenie told him, "Elmer, you have to go find work. We cannot stay in this condition for any longer. I will get well, and I will send for you if you will keep in touch with me and the authorities here. Please just go, and don't look back. I will be here when you come to get me, and I will be alive!"

Elmer, with tears in his eyes, held her tightly for a few minutes longer, then striding out of the building, he walked across the bridge onto the soil of America.

Wandering for a while through the city, trying to talk to store owners and blacksmiths, with his limited English, Elmer didn't make much headway. Finally, he found himself near the waterfront. He walked over to two work-hardened men and asked them in broken English if there were any jobs available. They turned and sized him up. The one, a sturdy fellow dressed in worn jeans and a flannel shirt, pointed to the dock where a weathered door opened into a building. He hurried there, and as he went through the door, he realized the smell of fish, and oil-soaked gear was the strongest he had smelled since landing.

Nearby was a man directing others in loading salt-covered fish into huge bins then pouring more salty brine over them. He waited until things settled down a minute then approached the man. After telling him carefully he needed work, the man pointed to another, dressed in dirty coveralls and wearing a filthy leather apron. This man spoke to Elmer in Dutch, the first time anyone had addressed him in his native language, and his knees felt weak with relief and joy to find someone from Holland.

After telling the man of his circumstance, he asked for a job. The man, who said he was Dave Lazenby, from England but had family in Holland, hired him on the spot. He was told where to start and where to get the leather apron, leather gloves, and heavy boots, and he almost ran to the shed where these items were dispensed, with their worth promised to be taken from his first month's wages.

Upon going to work that first day, Elmer thanked God for such a blessing and determined to be the best he could be until his sweet little Eenie could travel again. Although he was refused reentry onto the island, he wrote letters to her and was assured she would get them. He reminded her of her friend Catherine and to get well so they could travel to wherever she had gone with her husband out west, that there would probably be a job for him, and they could begin their lives in earnest once there.

Once traveling north, William studied his team of mules, two ragged-looking animals that had plenty of heart and strength despite their looks. Pulling willingly, the two mules took the couple north through the valleys, crossed several streams of water, and finally reached the point of land Bran had described in his letter of directions. Like an arrow, it pointed north, and along it went the wagon road, rough in places but worn down by many travelers.

After a week of careful travel, allowing the mules plenty of time to graze alongside any streams they encountered, they found a branch in the road. Bran's directions said to take the west branch from there where they would eventually reach the town of Indian Flats.

After another day's travel, coming over a pass on the foothills of the mountain, there before them lay the town. Catherine felt for William's hand, and as she held it, he squeezed her fingers, both agreeing there was special joy in that they had unerringly found their way nearer to where their boys were.

Bronwyn stared in amazement at the small town, growing and bustling with people. Pulling up the team by a livery stable on the edge of town, William helped Catherine down to stretch. Somehow, her thoughts went back to the sheriff, and she wondered if he ever came up here.

Walking inside, he found a friendly man working on a set of harness. Asking about the Emmerich ranch then remembering the man probably couldn't understand him, he wrote in English the name on a small piece of paper. He had practiced writing his name in English after the man in the blacksmith shop in New York had taught him how. Smiling, the fellow pointed west and signaled it was many miles.

When William didn't understand, the stable keeper signaled for him to follow him. Going outside, the man tipped his hat to Catherine and Bronwyn and headed up the street. William asked them to wait with the team and shrugging, followed the man. Into a building, he led William, where a typesetter was working. Speaking to him, he pointed at William and showed him the paper with the Emmerich name on it. The typesetter came around the machine and told William in Dutch where the ranch was at sixty miles west.

His face falling, William had thought the boys lived in or closer to Indian Flats. Then he realized the man could speak Dutch, and words poured out of him! Catching up on news from everywhere in the area, William was loath to leave his new friend. William learned a lot from the man in the newspaper office about the wagon road facing them, ranches along the way, and good water at the camping spots. Finally, knowing Catherine was waiting, he hurried back to reassure her that in a few more days' time, they would be reunited with their boys.

CHAPTER 12

On the wooden walkway, Catherine and Bronwyn linked arms and strolled up the street a ways. Bronwyn kept an eye out for a storefront that would serve her purpose for her own business. She hadn't yet told her parents about her plans; the only one knowing them was Branlen. She nudged her mother to a stop by a narrow building with a low eve in front, that looked about right for what she had in mind. She said, "Mother, I like the look of this little building. Isn't it cute? I wonder if someone owns it and what they use it for."

Catherine looked in the dusty window and replied, "It's empty and looks very dirty, cobwebs everywhere."

Bronwyn wondered how she could find out more without arousing her mother's suspicions but decided she could wait until another day.

As William approached, Bronwyn asked if they could stay in Indian Flats a few days, but William laughed and said no stopping yet. Someday, they would come back, but today, they were headed on. Only a few days lie between them and the boys, and they needed to get there.

As they came to live with Wade's parents on the ranch, tremendous peace and sense of wellness permeated their bodies. Henry had built a small cabin with two rooms for his parents down by the springhouse under a big black willow tree not far from his own home he and Mary lived in.

Mary was large with child and due to have the baby in a few weeks. Catherine was so thankful to have arrived before the birth. She knelt that first night with a prayer of thanks to their Maker for all of the blessings in their lives. She so wanted to help bring this first

American Emmerich into the world, and her prayers were now being answered.

The springhouse was built from short-cut logs with a roof of logs sodded with bark over a small spring of water, which bubbled up out of the ground icy cold and ran out the door and down into a pond a few dozen yards away. Split boards had been placed across the water, forming shelving to keep milk and dairy, butter, and meat well chilled. It was large enough for both families to use and made an excellent refrigerator. A textured small screen was nailed across some boards used to create a door, which could be kept closed on the cabinet and thus keep rodents, flies, and other nuisances out of the pans and bottles and off the hanging meat.

Inside the cabin, a fireplace was built in one end and a hand-hewn table and chairs made from cedar set in the center. Along the ceiling ran cottonwood beams, from which small articles could be hung or laid across to the next beam. An excellent place to store extra quilts, traveling bags, or any household item not used on a regular basis; even the round family bathtub could be placed up there. After all the months of travel and unsettled, exhausting worry about an uncertain future, when Catherine and William walked into the snug, comfortable little cabin, it looked like a castle to them. A spirit of love and safety enveloped them both, and they held each other and wept with joy.

Several small cupboards hung from the wall. A wooden flour bin William had carved for his wife in Holland, which they brought with them, filled with extra clothing, bedding, and a few other necessities, could sit under the cupboards. A second room was fashioned by a quilt strung across on a rope to give privacy to two beds attached to the walls with wooden pegs, and the springs were ropes drawn back and forth to form the base for feather mattresses. This made a fine albeit small room for Bronwyn, and Catherine placed handsewn quilts and warm covers on the beds. The floor was made of split cedar boards, and along one wall, a window made from isinglass looked out under the young black willow trees planted by William's sons in preparation for reuniting with their beloved parents and their sister.

━━━━►•◄━━━━

CHAPTER 13

Up in the mouth of the small canyon he named Spring Canyon, Jake had built his cabin near the bubbling spring that sprang out of the ground beneath a granite ledge and babbled its way on down the canyon. He was prospecting for gold he had been told was found a few miles east of their ranch. Jake had already dug a good tunnel, finding lead and silver and a few traces of gold but nothing substantial. He had more prospects he intended to develop later. He was a natural for a prospector, and the ore he discovered, he sold at a fair price, not enough to get rich but to make a decent living. As he prospected and staked claims, he built small cabins for shelter during the time he worked in the area. Therefore, later on, when Wade grew older, he would often come across one of these cabins and looking around, could find a nearby tunnel or diggings his uncle Jake had worked.

Jake loved guns and became an expert gunsmith, his talent in great demand across the territory. He loved carving the stocks, polishing the wood to a high gloss, and watching it develop into a long gun, which when placed against his cheek while aiming at something, felt smooth and soft, glistening with natural light brought out within the wood. He preferred fruitwood and decided to grow fruit trees with the idea in mind that when he used the trim from the trees, he also could use the delicious fruit they bore.

After his orchard was established some years later, he began grafting one type of fruit onto another tree and soon was growing several different apples on the same tree. He became well-known in the area as a pioneer in the business of grafting. He eventually took boxes of fruit carefully packed in the back of a wagon pulled by a team of mules to the town of Indian Flats, where he made a little money to help with his expenses. His mules were named Lucy and Bess, good-natured big mules that seldom got out of hand and if he needed to, he could ride. Although he didn't ride much and only used them to pull a wagon when he had ore or apples or beef from his brother's ranch to haul to town for sale.

One day, Jake decided to walk down to his father's home and take him and his mother, Catherine, a box of fruit. After picking from several trees, he packed the apples, apricots, and pears into a box lined with sacks. Tucking it under his arm and carrying his ever-present long gun, he latched the door to the cabin and began the hike down to William's.

Deep in thought about the next level in his tunnel and how to reach the ever-elusive silver lurking within, he finally smelled wood-smoke from the fireplaces and walked into the yard a few moments later. In front of his brother Henry's were two little girls playing and a little older boy sitting in the limbs of a tree. Yelling hellos and waving, they came tumbling down the walkway and into his arms. Quickly setting the box aside, he welcomed them with hugs and hellos. "What is my Libby doing today?" he asked as the little brown-eyed imp clung to his leg.

A tug on his beard brought his attention to another cute little girl slightly larger than Libby, with hair the color of burnt amber and eyes of sky blue. "And here is my Carrie!" Swooping her up, he swung her around to her intense joy and accompanied with shrieks of laughter. "Uncle Jake," asked little seven-year-old Wade, "did you bring a wildcat in that box? We heard one screaming last night, and Ben and I had to calm Eliza, Nettie, and the rest of this bunch down."

As Jake grinned his enjoyment of his nieces and nephew, a call from the cabin down under the black willows rang out. His mother, Catherine, had heard the commotion and stepped out on the porch. "Come on down, son, and tell us the news."

After a hug from his mother and giving her a squeeze back, Jake walked into her cabin and sat at the table. She set a cup of coffee in front on him and a plate that held three huge doughnuts sprinkled with sugar. Jake never had tasted anything as good as his mother's cooking in his life. Although he was a confirmed bachelor, he sometimes wondered if there was a woman in the world who could compare to his mother.

After a drink and a doughnut, he began telling her about the mine he was presently working on. Then he gave her a bag of mixed fruit from his trees and said yes, he had given a box to Henry's family.

The door opened as they visited, and in walked William, shortened and bent with time but still lively and busy with anything he could find to do. "Well, how is my boy doing? Find that gold yet?"

After getting a cup of coffee from Catherine, he sat down at the table and joined the visiting. He told Jake, "Early this morning, I walked down into the lower pasture and checked the water. I saw a cow outside the buck fence and wondered who she was. I climbed over the fence, and as I stepped down onto the ground, a rattler struck! He caught his fangs in my pants, and when I started kicking, the cursed thing hung on, and his body was swinging all over, trying to wrap around my legs, and I couldn't get free! My Lord, man, I thought I was dead.

"I kicked until I almost broke my leg, and finally, he came loose, and I climbed that fence so fast, I was like a cat! I jumped to the ground back in the pasture and checked to see if he had hooked me with those fangs, and nothing was wrong with me. I left that cow where she stood and walked up here as fast as I could. This isn't something an old man should be suffering!"

Jake tried not to laugh, but when his father began laughing, he joined in and laughed until tears came to his eyes at the picture in his mind! Catherine looked at them in amazement and finally said, "Yes, you laugh now, but you wouldn't be laughing if that snake had gotten his teeth into you!"

This brought on another round of laughter over the idea of a snake with teeth. Then Jake shuddered and said, "I can't even imagine such a thing."

CHAPTER 14

Sometime during that period, his grandmother bought a beautiful treadle sewing machine, and Wade seldom saw her away from it when he was a child. Catherine had made many quilts and bedding items and clothing by hand, which she took to Indian Springs and sold to earn funds for the sewing machine. She spent many hours sewing clothing for the entire family as she stated, "I need to earn my keep!"

He tried not to think about the past because both grandparents and parents were dead and buried in the plot of land on the ranch in the patch of cedars where his dear sister Eliza had been buried years before. He had loved them all dearly. But the memories always crowded into his mind, and they often brought much comfort, and Wade knew his memories shaped him into the man he had become.

An incident from his earliest childhood came to mind about his grandmother Catherine. His parents and grandparents had traveled into Indian Flats to purchase supplies for planting for the coming summer and had traveled in a wagon with low sides and one seat for the driver of the team. Wade was taken with them as he was five years old and wanted to go on the adventure. He nestled down in the wagon with his grandparents, who had taken quilts and piled them in the bed of the wagon upon which they sat.

When they got to the town, Mary and Catherine climbed down from the wagon with help from the men, and Mary, holding little Wade's hand, walked into the mercantile store. While the ladies were shopping for thread, fabric, and other necessities, William and Henry went out behind the store to the grain storage area to purchase grain seed.

Wade idled around, looking at the penny candy and new shoes on the shelves. Catherine couldn't speak English, and she found some fabric she liked but couldn't read the price on it. She took the bundle up to the front, where the heavyset woman who owned the store usually was, but she was nowhere to be found. From past experience, Catherine discovered the large woman would go into the back and fall asleep on a cot she kept there. A cowbell hung over the door attached to a rope would jingle and wake her up when a customer came in.

After looking around the store for a while, Catherine had gathered up several items. She placed them on the counter and taking the cloth, went outside the store to where the men were working loading grain seed. As she approached them, she asked in Dutch if Henry would come tell her the price of the cloth.

Suddenly behind her, a commotion broke out, and the woman came running, screaming, "Stop, thief!"

Accusing Catherine to be a thief shocked the entire group, including the woman's husband, Maxwell, who was selling the men the seed. He tried to calm his wife, who was shaking her fists and yelling until spittle flew onto Catherine's face. Not knowing English, Catherine had no idea why the ugly-natured shrew was screaming at her, but she was afraid and got behind her husband, William.

Finally, Henry got out of his mother why she had come outside the store with the cloth, which she had done to get a price on it. He tried to explain to the uncouth storekeeper but was told she would call the sheriff and that Catherine would be locked up, where all low-class people who couldn't speak English should go. That did it with Henry. He grabbed his wallet, slapped bills in Maxwell's hand, and took the cloth from his mother, where he dumped it on the ground in front of the irate woman. He then stalked over to where Mary had come, open-mouthed and staring, followed by Wade, who was taking in the entire scene in great detail. He told Mary, "Don't buy anything at all from this woman. We will drive to Texas before shopping here again."

Maxwell apologized for his wife's behavior, and as she began shouting again, he turned to her with an upraised hand. "Shut your mouth and don't open it again!"

The upset family gathered themselves into their wagon, and Henry headed the team toward home. Mary said, "Henry, we need supplies. There is another smaller store on down at the other end of town. Let's go there and at least get a few things we need."

Catherine said in Dutch to William, "What happened, and what did she say? And don't leave a word out!"

After William explained, Catherine said, "I just wanted to know the price of the cloth. For her to question my integrity because she was too lazy to get out of bed when she heard the bell above the door—I have never been so insulted in all my life!"

CHAPTER 15

As William talked with Catherine, Wade thought of what he had heard and seen and felt scared, angry, and defensive. As little as he was, he understood prejudice and bitterness toward those who were different. As he grew up, he understood it even better and realized the angry, selfish woman was not one to be changed, just pitied and left alone. In his mind, there was no help for someone like that.

One day in early spring, a rider arrived at the ranch from Indian Flats. This man brought a letter to Catherine from her former shipmate, Eenie. A frail tiny woman, Eenie had become ill on the crossing and had been kept in quarantine on Ellis Island as Catherine and William and Bronlyn had disembarked. Parting was painful, and Catherine often wondered if Eenie had survived. Now, here was a letter from her dear friend.

Opening the letter, she read,

> My dear Catherine,
>
> As you read this you may wonder if it is the voice from the dead. I am well, and recovered with the help of good nurses and good food. My dear husband Elmer found work, and I brought the children to him after three months of recovery on the Island. We lived in New York for a year, and Elmer kept his job. It paid nearly a dollar a day and we felt rich. We saved enough for a wagon and a team of mules, and now we are leaving the coast for the west. We signed up with

a wagon train bound for California, but we will leave it in Salt Lake City.

After we rest and recover from that, we would like to venture north into Montana Territory, as Elmer says William suggested we do this if we get that far. Presently we are in readiness to begin our trek west from Illinois. I pray daily for our safe journey, for our children, and for my husband and I to remain well. Also for our mules, who are cantankerous but strong, and we need them so desperately to stay that way.

I look forward to a letter from you to be waiting in Salt Lake City, Utah Territory, advising us as to the route we could take to get to you. I write this in deepest friendship and hope, with sincere good wishes from Eenie, Elmer and children.

Smiling, with tears in her eyes, Catherine hurried to the door, calling William. As he turned, she waved the letter. He stepped over to where she stood, and she shakily told him the contents of the letter. Grinning, he picked her up and twirled her around. "Your prayers on Eenie's behalf have been answered, Cath, and she and her family will be here to share in our life forever before we know it. Now, you get busy on a letter to her, and I better get the boys helping me build another cabin in preparation for their arrival!"

CHAPTER 16

Wade's childhood had been a privileged one in his way of thinking, since he had been raised on a cattle ranch miles from the closest town, and his family were his friends. Although they hadn't much money, they had plenty to eat and everything they needed when others were starving and getting thrown out of their rented houses in town because they had no jobs. A few times, members of their city family walked to the ranch for work or to borrow money because of the tough times living in town. When others had to have clothes for school and keeping up with town living, Wade and his family had what they needed for the ranch and to keep warm. Clothes were homespun, sometimes worn threadbare, and always handed down, but they had shoes and coats and were warm in winter.

Raising food in the garden, their mother, Mary, worked hard at preserving vegetables and to smoke and jerk their meat for preservation also. Making soap for washing clothes, soap for washing hands, candles for light in the evenings, and cutting and stacking wood for winter heat and year-round cooking took hours of daylight time.

Often by candlelight Mary and Catherine would be sitting by a candle or two, hand sewing garments, mending socks or shirts. Sometimes during summer, quilting frames would be set up outside near the black willow tree, and the women and girls—and boys too—would be recruited to help quilt several quilts. As Wade recalled those days, he remembered his arguments that he was a man and was needed on a horse more than on a stump tying a quilt! His mother just pointed to the stump he was to use, and that was that.

He laughed to himself; he rather got a kick out of tying the quilts but wouldn't let anyone else know it, especially his sister Carrie.

She seemed to have it in for him and always was watching for ways to torment him. He wanted to get even with her but just couldn't seem to catch her at her antics. She stuffed his boots with thistles one night, and another time, she set some mousetraps in his neatly stacked clothing. When he reached on the dresser to get a clean shirt once morning, two mousetraps clamped on two fingers. Yowling and jumping, he raced out of the bunkhouse and up to the main cabin, yelling, "Carrie," at the top of his lungs. Even the dogs barked at him. He couldn't prove it was her, but he knew it by the smug look on her face.

At least twice a year, they went to town in the wagon pulled by two stout workhorses when they paid their taxes and bought groceries for several months and necessities for tools, bolts of fabric, flour, and supplies they simply could not make for themselves. An adventure for the kids, Wade always looked forward to the trips to see other kids and what they did and where they lived.

In Indian Flats, his aunt Bronwyn had made her dream of owning a millinery come true. She had gone back to that small narrow building and after inquiries of several property owners, found the man who owned the little place. After negotiating for several hours, she convinced him to hear her words of increasing the growth in the town with an honorable profession. At first, the man sneered at her request of purchase. She said, "I intend to own a building and start my millinery with or without your building. However, you seem to think I am unable to handle a business and finances, so I will go to others until I get what I want to purchase. I have the money, and you will not get a penny of it."

As she turned to leave, he finally named a price she had been hoping for, and she looked at him with disdain in her eyes. Standing there, looking at him, he began to squirm, and said, "Okay, so you can have it at twenty-five dollars less."

Covering her shock, she quietly walked back to the table. Sitting down, she withdrew a document requiring his signature transferring his shop to her. He said, "You are prepared, aren't you?"

"Yes, I am. Do you sign or not?" As she spoke, she pushed the paper to him.

He grabbed a quill and, dipping it into the inkwell, signed his name and date. She handed him the money and turned to leave. The man stared at her and asked where she had come from. She smiled slightly and said, "From across the great ocean where you struggle every day to live."

When his parents decided that he and his mother and some of his brothers and sisters would move into the tiny town of Indian Flats on the north slopes of the mountain for school, he was both excited and worried. Hating to leave the ranch where he had spent his short life but looking forward to making new friends and seeing the world filled his thoughts. He didn't want to leave his father, Henry, and his dear grandparents alone on the ranch with just a couple of the older kids to help him. But the decision wasn't his to make, and he went with his mother and sisters and younger brothers to live in a one-room cabin in the town of Indian Flats for the winter so they could get some public education in the two-room log school.

Knowing Aunt Bronwyn was living nearby made the move into town easier. He loved and respected his lovely Aunt, who was so independent and intelligent. She was kind and loving to all her family and welcomed them all into her home at any time. At times, Wade wondered why she had never married but figured it was for the best as she could take care of herself as well as any man could.

Wade knew her story, that Sheriff Cramer had come into her little millinery store one day, surprising her speechless. He grinned at her and asked her to go have lunch with him up the street to the Broken Spoke restaurant. They talked long after the meal, and one day led to another until she knew she had fallen in love with the sheriff, and he with her. They planned a summer wedding, and she worked at sewing a wedding dress with the help of her mother and grandmother. Then one night, a drunken miner staggered out of a saloon, shooting his gun into the air. Yelling and jumping from unseen threats, the drunk was having hallucinations. Sheriff Cramer stepped out of the office and caught a stray bullet square in the chest. The town doctor tried to help but declared him dead within minutes.

Bronwyn was shattered and thought her life would end as well. She folded her wedding dress and at the cemetery, before the coffin was lowered into the earth, carefully and with dignity, laid it upon the casket. Somehow, she kept breathing and after the funeral, went into her shop with a frenzy of grief, anger, and pain. She wore black for years, and when she began getting her bearings on her future, she brought her shop to the forefront of Indian Flats and refused any attention from men from then on. She had buried her love with her sweetheart, Dawson Cramer.

Wade knew she loved riding and always wore a proper riding skirt with buttoned top and long sleeves, complete with a short hat affixed on her head like a crown. She never rode slowly either. He loved watching her run her horse through the ridges full speed, racing him when he rode with her, then coming quietly down the street when she reached town. She carried a short gun tucked inside her small valise that was never far from her. Also, once she told him that she carried a long knife tucked inside a scabbard tied around the inside of her upper leg. Not a thing a lady would do, but who was to know? And she said, with her eyes sparkling, anyone who found out about it would find out when it was used on them. She laughed and told him that was her best insurance for protection in a tough situation.

CHAPTER 17

As far as his memory took him, he remembered most of the people from the little town being nice to them and the kids treating them all right. Some people were kinder than others, and his mother made friends that lasted her lifetime and his too. They rented an old log cabin on the north end of the little town that seemed all right for their purposes. Although there were seven kids and their mother, they made do, and the cabin kept them sheltered from storms. Learning where dead cedars were in the nearby hills and hauling loads of wood with a borrowed wagon and team for the stove in the corner of the cabin, they prepared for winter. Handling an axe was a skill the older kids had, and his mother, Mary, had chopped plenty of wood in her life. They discovered hauling wood for the school helped pay a required fee for the teacher.

During this time, his mother, Mary, worked to help ladies through their pregnancies and helped as a midwife in their delivery. She also did handsewn collars for dress tops; lovely, delicate handkerchiefs; and other hand sewing. She was able to trade for or purchase their food while living in the town with this talent, and she also sewed for Bronwyn's millinery. Her sewing received great acclaim, and travelers from other communities often stopped in the millinery for her goods.

He learned some pranks and new skills from the kids but nothing really bad. One day at school, a buddy said, "Hey, Wade, let's have a little fun with old Mr. Stiff Britches! There's a ladder going into the attic in the school wash bench closet. We can climb up into the attic and from there, look down through a knothole. That walking stick of a teacher will be getting things ready for afternoon class! Come on! This will be fun! Grab some pebbles!"

When the teacher walked beneath them, Enoch dropped a pebble. It landed on the teacher's shoulder. He flinched then glanced around, looking for the culprit who was throwing things at him. Smothering their laughter, the boys got another stone ready. The kids all came filing back inside, and before the teacher could miss them, they launched another rock. This one hit the teacher's nose and knocked his glasses off. They scurried down the ladder and came walking in the door while the teacher held his nose and cursed children in general. The slow-witted teacher never did figure that one out.

One time, his sister Eliza was on the playground after lunch, and some big boys began bullying little Harry. Only in first grade, he couldn't manage to hold on to his lunch sack and get dragged around the yard, so he let go, and the older boys took it, jeering at him all the while. Unknown to them, Eliza walked up behind them and swung her little purse as hard as she could squarely onto the one boy's back. It almost knocked the breath out of him, and as he turned, gasping, she hit him solidly in the nose with her fist. Backward he staggered, blood pouring out of both nostrils, and ran as fast as he could for the water tap.

The other boy left in a hurry, dropping little Harry's lunch sack, ripped, with the apple and baked potato rolling in the dirt. Eliza smiled at Harry, saying, "Gather up your lunch, and let's go wash off the apple. You can peel the potato skin and get rid of the dirt on it and still eat it. Hurry now so you won't be late to go back inside for afternoon classes."

Wade held his sisters in great regard and for the most part, loved them dearly. Sometimes, one of them would get on his last nerve, and then the dust, his hat, and pigtails would fly. His brothers and he could settle things with shoving or pushing or a wild wrestle; however, with a sister, it was quite different.

One afternoon, he wasn't feeling good after school, so when he got to the cabin, he lay down on the bunk and fell asleep. When he woke up, little Carrie had painted his face with a matchstick dipped in their mother's bluing used for freshening up colors in clothes while washing. Not discovering it until supper and everyone around the table, when the others began laughing, he raced to the mirror. He felt he wanted to catch a skunk and shove it under her quilt that night. It would have been worth the stink to see her gag. So that night, deciding a skunk would make him just as sick as Carrie, he snuck to her bed and with a pair of scissors, cut her hair short in the back and up the sides until she looked like a little boy.

They all endured shrieks and screams in tones ranging from low to high the next morning. Wade raced for school without breakfast and arrived there before the teacher. When the sober-faced man arrived to open the door, he was surprised to see Wade dash inside ahead of him and take his place at his desk, keeping his head down. The teacher loudly requested Wade to look at him when he spoke to him, and when Wade raised his head, he saw the usually sour teacher's face break up in a snicker at the blue-faced kid seated before him.

Shortly, the rest of the class arrived, including Carrie with her new haircut. Stomping in, she strode up to Wade's desk and pointing a small finger, informed him her haircut was just what she needed. She would set a new trend, and all the girls would want their hair cut that way. She did look somewhat like a pixie, an angry one at that.

However, she informed him no one was going to want their face painted a pale blue! His reply to that was that they would just think it was a tattoo, and all the boys would want one.

Meanwhile, Mother Mary arrived and quietly informed the teacher to keep a lid on the class and her children. They were experimenting with designs and trends for the turn of the century, and she wouldn't expect ridicule or further aggravation from an educated adult. She was certain he would be able to write a paper in the near future of his class's attempts to create acculturation and perhaps receive acclamation from his peers.

Turning toward the door, Mary glanced at Wade and Carrie long enough to convey a warning of behavior and a reckoning after school with her. Head held high, Mary left a stunned and bewildered teacher, wondering how he was going to get through to the end of this challenging year in Indian Flats.

— •⬤• —

CHAPTER 18

While in Indian Flats, Wade and his brothers and sisters didn't need a horse to get to school, but other kids living five or six miles from town did, so the fathers of those children built a stable behind the one-room school, where the horses were unsaddled, fed some hay, and tied up for the day. Outside was a water trough, where the kids could water their horses before heading home.

After his fifth year in school with summers at the ranch, he left school to work on the ranch and never attended school after that. He always felt he could have done more in his life had he received a proper education, but he did well enough for the times he lived in.

He found he could read as well as any of his peers in school and loved reading a good book in the evening by the light of the coal oil lamp. He had a fast and intelligent mind that when he was asked to estimate the weight of a steer or bull or horse, he could come within a few ounces. Always wanting the ranch and cattle with riding horses to break and good workhorses to pull the hay wagon, his mind and physical strength were spent in that direction.

One January, when winter winds howled and snow blew across the western ranges, cattle were snowed in and ranches isolated. During a lull in the weather, Wade and his brother Ben each saddled their best and strongest horses, and each leading a packhorse laden with corn and barley, headed across the upper pasture and through the gate to where the cattle had last been seen on winter range. After an hour of breaking trail, Wade turned it over to Ben and fell into place behind him, giving his horse a rest.

Traveling half a day west, they finally began seeing cows, some scattered but alive. They began calling to them and kept riding. Well into the afternoon, they had discovered most of the herd and began riding in a large circle, calling all the time. As the cows approached, they took turns getting off and carrying fifty-pound sacks of feed to the circle their horses had tromped down and began feeding the grain. The cattle fell into line behind them, some running alongside, trying to lick the feed as it spilled out of the sack. Knowing they had a long, cold ride still to get back to the ranch, as soon as the last sack of grain was emptied, they mounted their horses and rode for home.

This was a normal winter for the boys, raising cattle in the northwestern territories. Establishing a ranch and opening up farmland from cedars and sagebrush weren't easy work. Cutting posts for fences and clearing stumps, rocks, brush, and other debris took all hands.

Always fencing private property boundaries and separating some areas for pastures, Wade and his brothers and their father, Henry, kept busy. Often, his grandfather William helped put up buck fence. They would cut trees and trim all the limbs back and then beginning with some larger trunks, lay limbs across diagonally, then flat, and then sticking some in straight up. It was a matter of weaving, not with cloth but with wood. When they went along the fence line with this method, the fence stood up to winter snows, summer rains, and strong winds with no staples or wire. Cattle couldn't get through the buck fence, and horses left it alone too. A hundred years later, Wade's descendants saw parts of the old buck fence in areas of the ranch.

Wade's sense of humor sometimes backfired. He knew his brother Ben was going up to change the water on the field in the upper pasture, and the alfalfa was growing quite tall. Ben's fear of snakes was legendary, and there were many rattlers around on the ranch. When watering, they all had to keep a sharp eye on the ground and listen for the rattle of warning the snakes usually gave. However, if a snake's rattles got wet, he couldn't rattle, and so watchfulness led to safety.

Wade ran up the trail and looking around, found a place in the alfalfa near where Ben would be coming to divert the water at the dam in the creek. He flattened himself in the tall crop and held a long stick in his hand stretched out to where Ben would be shoveling.

Presently, Ben came along, whistling and carrying the shovel across his shoulder. Walking over to the dam, he began shoveling. With his back to where Wade lay hidden, Wade knew he could really get him, so he reached out his stick and poked Ben in the back of the leg, while hissing loudly though his lips.

Ben went into the air and swung the shovel as hard as he could, narrowly missing Wade's head and neck. Wade rolled over and laughed so hard, he couldn't breathe, then he caught a number 12 boot as is landed in his ribs. Ben dove on top of him and pounded him with his fists, blind with terror from the thought of a rattler sinking its fangs into the back of his leg and then seeing his brother, the practical joker, laughing his brains out at his expense. The day hadn't turned out quite as funny as Wade had intended as on his walk back to the house, nursing a bloody nose and sore ribs, he realized too late the danger he had put himself in with Ben's shovel-wielding arms and righteous anger. The family had been taught to never hold grudges, but this took some time to recover from for both brothers.

CHAPTER 19

While herding cattle across the trails along the mountains and across the foothills from one grazing area to another, in the summer, it was long and tedious work. One hot summer day, Wade, Ben, their dad, and Nettie were following a herd of seventy or so cows through some brush, quaking aspen, and scrub oak. Wade, being bored to death, found an old prospector's pan lying half buried in the dirt near the trail. Jumping off his horse, he broke a dead limb from a nearby tree and began banging on the pan with all his might. The entire herd of cows jumped as one and began a wild-eyed tail-over-the-back all-out stampede along the bench. As they reached a steep draw, most turned and raced down it entirely off the trail.

Henry began swearing, and spurring his horse, he tried to break up the bunch and at least keep part of them on the bench. Wade swung aboard his horse and about broke his neck racing along the edge of the draw until he found a way down. The only thing he could do was follow until the draw emptied out onto a flat below nearly a mile from the trail. Swinging wide around the slowing herd of panic-stricken cows, Wade waved his hat and yelled to circle them. Tiring, they stopped and stared at him like they'd never seen a rider before. Talking and yelling, threatening and cajoling, Wade gathered what he could and headed them around the bottom to where another canyon came in and he could finally get them going up it to the bench above. He wondered if cows could think and what they thought! Deciding to not laugh in front of his dad and brother and sister, he grinned all the way to the trail at the top of the canyon.

During those long days herding and handling the cattle, the boys found ways to entertain themselves, and their dad hoped they wouldn't be so crazy. Ben began roping sagebrush, next a cow dog, and then the occasional calf just for fun. He began slow with his roping, but as the years progressed, Ben became the best roper on the ranch. He could make a lariat dance. Ben began swinging the rope around his horse's head and shoulders and finally walked his horse entirely through the loop, keeping the lariat swirling and flying. Wade loved watching this, and although he tried it, he found he had no patience to perfect it like Ben. After nearly knocking his saddle horse's ears off with his rope, he quit trying.

At a Fourth of July in Indian Flats, Ben put on a show with his lariat and best horse, bringing the audience to their feet with applause. After dismounting, Ben began twirling the rope around his head and began a dancing two-step. As he danced about, the rope came down over his shoulders and around his body, and he stepped inside then out of the loop. People loved seeing him handle the rope with such grace and dexterity, and many young ladies wished he would circle them within the loops of his lariat. Youngsters spent hours of the day trying to swing the rope like Ben.

Wade loved horse racing and spent many times with his brothers and friends seeing whose horse could outrun his Quarter Teacup So. At a celebration in Indian Flats, a group of young men decided to hold a horse race and invite all the townspeople to come watch.

Davie Clay told the others, "Let's bet on the winner and get the word out. Somebody will make a bundle!"

Word quickly spread, and a friend, Cole Shipman, agreed to hold the purse. Wade bet high on Quarter Teacup So. Shortly, it was time for the race. The mayor of the town, known for opinionated decisions, announced the race would be a relay, where the men would form teams, and each team begin with one man, saddling, riding, and upon reaching the designated spot, jump off and unsaddle. His partner would then repeat the pattern until the first team to reach the end wins.

Wade looked at his brothers and friends. They quickly began deciding who would be on their team, but the mayor again stepped in and announced there would be a drawing for teams. Tempers flared, and a couple of racers walked away.

Wade determined to stay in, and as his team was selected, he drew a few good men with fast horses. Cole Shipman was on his team and told him, "Wade, if you get to my horse, she won't take spurs. Don't spur her!"

Agreeing, Wade got in place, knowing his little bay gelding could outrun nearly anything and hoped fervently he could use him. But as luck would have it, as the horses were run, when his turn came up, he got Cole's mare. He ran for the saddle, threw it on and didn't cinch it up, just drawing the latigo through the D ring on the cinch, jumped aboard and holding the latigo in his hand, took off. As he went, he hit her with his spurs, completely forgetting the warning. The mare went straight up and twisted, coming down bucking furiously. The latigo strap burned between his fingers, the saddle flew off with him on it, and the mare went running off on her own. Wade sat there astride the saddle, feeling like a fool and inwardly cursing himself. Jeering laughter from the other riders got him to his feet, and sweeping his hat off, he performed a grand bow to the audience.

✦ ● ✦

CHAPTER 20

As Wade sat there on the edge of the desert, reflecting on his life and the ranch, he realized that thinking backward wasn't the direction he wanted to go, so he put his thoughts on the future. Raising a good breed of Hereford cattle and keeping the ranch going were his main goal. With aging parents and old grandparents living there, along with six siblings not yet married, Wade knew he had a lot of work to accomplish to keep the ranch prospering and make it pay all of them.

As he sat his horse, the beautiful bay gelding with four stocking feet shook its head and blew softly. Wade realized the rain clouds were moving his direction with the scent of sweet rain mixed in the sage, so gathering up the reins and gently kneeing the horse into a walk, going through sage and cedars on the trail, he headed for the ranch off in the distance.

One of his younger brothers approached Wade one morning while Wade was in the corral with a young horse, working with it and calming it down. Ben spoke quietly so as not to spook the little horse. "Hey, Wade, what do you think about building some corrals along the mountain and catching some wild horses? We could break them and sell the ones we don't want to keep and make some spending money!"

Wade thought a moment and realized the idea was a good one. "I'd like that. Do you think the other boys would like to help?"

"Some of them would for sure. After breakfast, let's ask Harry. I don't think Dan would want to do it because he don't like to ride on an open road, let alone tear through the ledges and cedars chasing those mustangs!"

As Wade put the little stud away, the idea grew on him, and he felt excitement growing for such an adventure.

The boys and the rest of the family sat down to their mother's delicious breakfast of eggs, homegrown and smoked pig meat, huge slices of homemade bread and freshly churned butter, with a platter of sliced tomatoes picked that morning and washed and sliced by sixteen-year-old Carrie. Wade had heard chickens protesting their nests being raided that morning as little sister Libby had searched out and collected eggs from hens that ran free all summer and nested beneath sagebrush, rabbitbrush, and around the haystacks. Two pitchers of milk from their milk cow were taken from the springhouse under the black willow tree, where all the perishables were kept in screened-in cupboards built over the top of a spring of fresh water, which ran out the door and on down through a small meadow and into a pond. The family might be short on money but never on food.

As the family was eating the hearty breakfast, Wade looked at Ben, who had approached him earlier with the horse-catching idea, and slightly nodded. Ben leaned back in his chair and said with enthusiasm, causing his voice to crack, "Guess what me and Wade are going to do?"

Mother sharply looked at Ben and said, "Watch your language, young man! That's 'Wade and I.' You might be living on this isolated ranch, but you will speak properly and use good English!"

Chastised, Ben apologized for his slang and went on with his story. "Anyway, if Harry would help, we could build good corrals and wings into them, and we could bring whole herds of wild horses into them!"

As the boys thought this over, their dad said that he figured that would be a good way to make a little extra income for the entire family. The mountain held many herds of horses running wild, and catching some wouldn't hurt at all. It might help in the long run as the grass could be used for cattle or sheep with addition to the small permits they now had. As far as running a herd into a small corral, that would never do. Small bunches of eight or ten would be easier to work with. And the older studs and mares could be cut out easily.

As the family discussed this new idea, enthusiasm built, and many suggestions were brought up. As Ben had said, the oldest brother, Dan, emphatically stated he had no interest in such a venture and wanted no part in it. He would rather work on the fields, getting brush cut out and ready for planting. Even digging ditches for the canyon creek water held more interest for him than riding a horse.

So the following morning found Wade, Ben, and Harry riding up Sandy Creek canyon, looking for the perfect place to build a corral to catch the wild horses. Dan stayed at the ranch to tend to some watering that needed to be done on dry pastures. At last, there was a low pass, with a well-used horse trail coming off the pass from the head of a long draw named Brush Creek, choked with cedar, mahogany, and buckbrush. Across the draw and between the granite ledges led the trail, showing the boys the horses frequented the area, coming down the steep slopes for water in the main canyon. Stepping off their saddle horses and tying them up, they hefted axes and shovels and began looking at the corral site.

Harry said, "Let's begin by the granite ledge and swing down through the cedars with a long wing above to direct them into the corral. Once they're running, they won't look for a place to escape, and when they're inside, one of us can slide poles across the opening."

The other boys agreed.

Cutting trees and setting posts took most of the day as they made a stockade fence. Sun setting, they wearily placed tools by a cedar, climbed on their horses, and headed back to the ranch.

That night, around the table, they reported their progress. Henry wondered if the corral was big enough. Ben replied that if they made it too large, the horses could get a run at the fence and try to jump it. The stockade fence blocked a lot of their view and helped keep them from trying to jump. Wade said, "We probably need reinforcements around the top of the fence, so we will take some pipe from the mine down below and tie it along the top."

Early morning, the boys began their trip back up the canyon to the side draw, where they had begun the corral. This time, they worked on the pipe at the top of the stockade, and when it was finished, they began the wing. It was hidden until the horses were well into it, and then they would be herded into the corral below before they could react.

Pleased with their work, the boys again headed back to the ranch, discussing ways they could get behind the herd on the top slope and spook them down. They would need Harry to hide near the opening and slide poles behind the herd as they entered the corral.

After a good night's sleep, they rode to the corral and showed Harry where to hide in a tree by the poles that had been carefully notched and placed. The two other brothers rode up Sandy Creek to the top, circled around, and scanned the area for the wild herd.

Wade whispered, "There they are about a mile over in the head of Brush Creek, right where we want them!"

So checking their cinches, they trailed across several canyons and into the drainage above where they'd last seen the horse. "There! Below! They're beginning to run!"

As Harry's voice echoed, the boys hit leather hard and raced to get the bunch going into the canyon, not out of it as the wise old stud was trying to lead them. Horses running full out, the young cowboys headed the wild herd, and down into the brush-choked draw they went, ropes waving, shouts and pounding hooves scaring the wild horses into an all-out run down the trail they had followed for years. Over granite outcroppings, through scattered patches of granite sand, and tearing through the cedars, dust flying high and with little mountain-grown ponies beneath them, boys and mounts raced down the canyon, chasing their wild horses into the corral below.

As they hit the head of the wing, Wade began to shout, "Harry, get the poles across!"

As Wade shouted, he made a flying dismount and ran to help Harry slide the poles. Suddenly, it was over. Wild-eyed, stomping, snorting horses inside the corral. Blowing, lathered ponies on the outside. Cowboys like none other, laughing and pounding each other on the back. Glad for a job well done.

CHAPTER 21

While letting their horses get their breath and cool off, the boys walked around the corral, checking for weak spots and admiring the horses inside. Wade chose his pick immediately in a long-legged sorrel stud about two years old with a white strip down his face. Each of the others chose a favorite, and then they mounted up for the ride back.

Discussing how they would get the horses they'd chosen to the home corral, Wade said, "Why don't we bring mules up with a harness and a singletree and rope the ones we want and tie each of them to the tugs on a mule's singletree?"

Ben replied, "Just turn the mules loose, and they will bring the broncos home and teach them to lead at the same time! After they have gone, we can turn the rest loose."

So it was decided, and in the cool of the next morning, the boys took lariats and began roping their choices to keep. After a lot of dust and hot, tiring work, there were three wild ponies tied to the singletrees at the back of three mules' harnesses.

The stoic mules were strong enough to keep the mustang youngsters' wild antics under control and pull them along as the boys turned them loose one by one, to start dragging loads of fighting horse flesh home.

After a bit, they opened the pole gate, and spooked the herd on out and up the draw from where they'd come. When the horses reached the top of the canyon, the old stallion's whistle could be heard as he paused and challenged the world of man.

Storing the tools beneath a granite outcropping until they could come back and get them, the boys got on their horses and followed mule tracks down the draw, into the main canyon, and down the trail toward the ranch. When they came into sight of the ranch, standing in the wing down by the corrals were the three mules, each with a ragged wild pony still attached to their singletrees.

Grinning at each other, the boys rode up and opened the gate into the main corral. When the mules were safely inside with their still-resisting partners, the boys gathered up ropes and halters, untied the singletrees, and proceeded to work each horse into somewhat submission into another smaller corral. Leaving halters on, they untied the ropes and let the wild ponies settle down and get a drink of water from the trough.

This was a typical self-sufficient part of life in Wade's existence so far and nothing out of the normal, just doing a job that needed to be done and taking advantage of the opportunity to add to the ranch horse number, easing reliance on all the ranch horses and their workload of riding the mountain trails gathering and placing cattle.

There were visitors to the ranch quite often during summer months, and although the ranch was in a remote locality in Western Montana, the wagon trail provided access to the family going and coming. Cousins from town would ride out or drive their team and wagon out and stay a couple of weeks, and there would be fun for all the kids in that. Sometimes, strangers would stop in as they traveled through the country, and Mary and Catherine would always feed them and make sure they had food to take with them when they left.

One sunny spring morning, Mary said to Catherine, "Let's get the fires going and heat water for the washing, and I will get bread mixed, and while we are doing the wash, we'll bake bread. We'll be outside most of the day, and the stove in the kitchen won't make us so hot."

So the huge kettle was taken down and placed next to the fire-pit, where the women started a fire. Then enlisting little daughters' help, buckets of water were carried from the well, and when the fire was going just right, the kettle was put on top of the rocks around the pit, and water poured into it until it was nearly full. As Catherine trudged back and forth from the well with her granddaughters and buckets of the water, she thought how much work it was to do the laundry for the family. But it was satisfying work, and the clothes smelled so good hanging on the lines. And she loved her daughter-in-law with all her heart. How thankful she was to have such a lovely person as Mary in her life, and how happy she was that Henry had found her. Catherine thought of how Henry and Mary had met and smiled at the thought.

Thinking of family and working on laundry, Catherine realized the dresses they wore daily were heavy material able to hold up to work. However, dressier dresses were not so easy to maintain with all the lace, ribbons, rows handmade covered buttons, and flounces; washing them carefully, then ironing all that took hours of work. The men wore canvas pants and heavy shirt, but for church or special occasions, they had jackets and ties and billowy-armed white shirts that required extra care in the laundry and ironing. She smiled to herself, thinking of how a woman's work was never done and that many hands made work light.

As Henry Emmerich had traveled across the ocean on the great ship, he had been unaware of the lovely Mary Gibbons and her family, and the pair had not met until they arrived in New York. As they were going through Ellis Island, Henry saw the most beautiful girl he had ever seen, and as he stared, her gaze met his. She smiled slightly, tipped her head, and walked past him with her mother. Henry wondered if the family would stay in New York, knowing he was bound for the west. Henry thought of her often as he crossed the plains, arriving in Salt Lake City, Utah, some months later.

One morning, the door to their cabin opened, and his friend he shared the cabin with came in, excited and waving a piece of paper. "Henry, come here and sit while I tell you some wonderful news! I was outside working on a harness for the blacksmith, and a man stopped by and asked me if I had plans to settle anywhere in particular. I told him you wanted farmland and a ranch and would go wherever you had to go to get it.

"He then told me there is land in Montana Territory, and he would like to invest in it himself, but he works for the railroad being built across America and can't leave this area right now. I think Montana Territory could be a great opportunity for you. I don't want any part of anymore bad weather, and am headed for California as soon as I can make enough to get myself there. What do you think?"

Henry said, "I think I am ready for a change and anything to get out of this city. Where is the man, and what is his name?"

Catherine thought of the results of that meeting, which had ended in Henry's taking a contract with Mr. Charles Gibbons to freight timber back to Salt Lake City from Montana Territory. Mr. Gibbons would invest in the operation with his own money in that he would buy the freight wagon and team to begin the contract Henry signed.

After the meeting, Mr. Gibbons had invited Henry and his friend to his home for dinner. When they arrived, they found a two-story log home with a large front room and dining table taking up most of the lower story. As the family entered the house, Mrs. Gibbons graciously welcomed them and began introducing her family to theirs. As the family began introductions, Henry found himself choked with emotion. There standing before him was the lovely girl he had last seen at Ellis Island. She recognized him too and smiled sweetly.

As preparations began for his new job taking him north to Montana Territory, Henry wondered if he dared to believe that someday in the future, he and Mary Gibbons might become a team. Knowing only time would tell, he softly spoke to Mary before he left that night and told her he hoped that someday, they would meet again. She smiled and quietly told him he could count on it. Catherine remembered the joy in Henry's eyes as he described his wedding day to her.

CHAPTER 22

In June, the fields yielded their first crop of alfalfa, and work began for the men to cut, rake, and haul the huge amount of hay to the stackyards where it would be stored for winter feed for the livestock. One morning, the boys and their father had gathered out by the blacksmith shop where Henry and Dan were working on a broken mowing machine tooth. Sharpening it and keeping the fire going in front of the bellows, they didn't hear the riders coming.

Wade stepped into the yard with his hammer in his hand, and there were three men sitting their horses, looking at them. Wade said, "Hello. Get down and rest your horses."

Nodding their heads, they dismounted. Wade noticed they weren't dressed like cowboys. They had dressier pants on, wore jackets and ties, and had small hats on their heads that Wade liked to call "town hats." When Henry and Dan came out of the blacksmith shop, Henry asked them, "What can we do for you?"

The one fellow who appeared to be the boss replied, "We have been covering these mountains for several years, trying to find the bootleggers running booze around here, and there is evidence that there is a bunch holed up in this area. Have you people seen anything of them?"

Henry shook his head and said, "I haven't seen them or any sign of their stills. Do you know what they look like?"

About that time, a fellow came sauntering around the shed from the direction of the upper field, carrying a pitchfork and wearing a wide-brimmed straw hat. Wade stared at him as he walked up to the group and stood by Henry's elbow with an affable grin on his face. Wade stared. Henry hardly looked at the man and went on talking to the three who had introduced themselves as US Marshalls hunting bootleggers.

As the talk wound down, the three law officers mounted their horses and headed out the gate. Wade was dumbfounded. Here was a bootlegger he knew who had walked in, smart as he pleased, to listen to the conversation and get any information he could while posing as a hired hand of the Emmerichs. Henry turned, looking at the bootlegger, and said in a voice tight with anger, "Get off my land and don't come back. You'll get my ranch taken away. I told you a long time ago I don't want liquor around my family, and if you left me and my family alone, I'd leave you alone. Now you've ended all that. If I hear of you camped in these ridges and canyons, anywhere, I'll burn you out myself! Now git!"

Wade thought it the funniest thing he'd ever seen—and the most daring. As he began laughing, he got a glare from his father. Turning away, Henry fought to keep from laughing himself, knowing it wouldn't do to let his sons think he thought it funny. But Wade did talk to his brothers, who all got a laugh out of it. Then between them, they decided they better visit the bootleggers and get a taste of that moonshine before they left the country with it.

As soon as Wade, Ben, and Dan got a chance, they rode across the foothills to where the still was set up, hidden in a little draw near a spring and under a canopy of oaks. As they drew near, one of the bootleggers stepped out, holding a rifle loosely pointed toward the boys boots. When Wade spoke, the man grinned and welcomed them into the camp. "I thought your eyes were going to pop from your head, young fellow," the outlaw said, who had worn the straw hat and walked too boldly into the conversation at the ranch.

Before long, a grand time was spent sampling the liquid inside the small hooped barrel lying sideways on some logs. Before they got too far gone, Wade told his brothers, "Let's get going. Now, boys, how about a barrel of that stuff to take with us?"

Obligingly, as payment for their silence, the outlaws handed up a barrel, about the perfect fit behind a saddle, and after tying it on with latigo leathers, the boys rode back toward the ranch.

Agreeing their father and young Harry could never know, they found a perfect forked cedar just out from the ranch, where they placed the barrel to age as it rocked in the breeze and be there when they needed a little white lightning! It didn't take long for Harry to figure out what was up with his older brothers, and after a little listening in on conversations, he decided to take a hike to see if he could track his brothers back to where the barrel hung. Sure enough, he found the keg and climbing the tree, carefully removed it. Walking on rocks and stepping in grass, he found another tree some distance away and climbed up to its forks where he hid the forbidden treasure.

Of course, he sampled it and after properly choking on the strong liquid, decided it was just right to cut the dust in his throat after hauling hay all day. His walk a little unsteady, he slipped back to the ranch and felt quite proud of himself to pull the wool over older brothers' eyes.

After a day or so, Wade headed out to his cedar cache. Nothing there! After searching the tree and area around it thoroughly, Wade determined it had been stolen. Now this was serious business, and if it was one of his brothers, he could deal with him. However, what if a stranger found it?

He went back home and collared Dan. He denied having anything to do with it and was just as irate as Wade over it. They decided it must be Ben since he had done most of the drinking at the boot-legger camp. When Ben came back from moving some cows into a pasture with better feed, his brothers were waiting. It didn't take long to decide none of them had done it.

So Wade took off, and after hiking to the tree where he had left the keg, he got on his hands and knees and started tracking. Here was an imprint and there, a partial heel print. Grass crushed and a rock turned over, he was suddenly at the base of another large cedar. Jumping to his feet, he looked up, and there swinging in the forks was the keg. Up the tree he climbed, gathered the keg up like a baby in his arms, and swung down from the branches.

This time, no one would find it! Making a circle even closer to the ranch, walking in his sock feet, and carrying his boots, he found another tree. Up into the forks went the keg but not before Wade had a long pull at the spigot on the bottom. Walking the rest of the way home in sock feet, he pulled his boots on outside the gate. Watching for furtive looks from his brothers, he saw nothing suspicious until he saw Harry looking at him with narrowed eyes the next morning. He grinned and saluted Harry and walked off. No one found the keg after that, and he wouldn't let on to Ben or Dan he had found it until its contents were nearly gone.

The enjoyment of moonshine spilled over into the love of a good party in the mining town of the New Guinea. Located up in the canyon of a mountain range about forty miles east of Indian Flats, miners had found several strikes, and two or three had made their fortune. During its heyday, New Guinea was a wide-open town with little law and few morals.

Young Harry was welcomed with open arms into the saloons as long as his pockets were full. When he was in a drunken stupor and near passing out, he would be placed in a back room to sleep it off. Sometimes upon awakening, his pockets were empty, and he had no way of knowing if he had drank it all up or if he had been rolled during the night.

After a few days of carousing, he headed home to the ranch, broke and full of regret. It was in the early hours of morning just after midnight when he arrived, put his horse up, and headed for the bunkhouse. Taking off his dirty clothes, he stripped down to his white long handles. Then looking at his bunk, he decided he was about to choke to death for want of a drink of water, so he hiked up in the field above the house where the spring was and a cold pipe full of water ran into a little pond. Kneeling down at the edge of the pipe, he began drinking.

Suddenly, from the knoll above the spring came the sound of running feet and gasping, growling coyotes. He reared up to his knees then onto his feet and taking one look, thought he was surely dead as they seemed to be rabid. He turned and ran for the bunkhouse as though the seven hinges of hell were after him.

In the moment of his rearing up, the hound dogs from the ranch were merely arriving back from some night escapades and heading to the spring for a drink too. They took one look at the tall white ghostly apparition lunging upward from the grass, turned tail, and fled as fast as their legs could carry them. They arrived at the top of the knoll about the same time Harry arrived at the bunkhouse, where they bayed half the night. The next morning, they came carefully into the yard, watching furtively around for whatever had nearly killed them in the night.

One day while riding, Harry told Wade his story, and Wade laughed until he almost fell off his horse.

CHAPTER 23

One early morning Wade told Ben as they were getting dressed for their day in the bunkhouse, "Let's ride to the east pasture in Dan's canyon and gather the cattle and take them over the ridge to where there is better grass and the water is running a little more. That spring was cut way back, and I'm afraid it will quit before we are over there again. We don't want a bunch of cows going without water in this heat."

Ben readily agreed, and the boys headed for the house for breakfast with their folks.

After talking over the day's plans with their dad, Henry, and the rest of the family and each deciding their plan for the day, Wade and Ben went to the corral where they caught their cow horses and got them saddled. Riding east for a few miles, they came upon the short, broad canyon where the cattle were scattered out feeding. Down the center of the canyon, it was wide and open, with good grass and a creek running through it. A fire some years before had opened it up, and the grass did well with no competition from the cedars. There were still a few tall stumps from the dead trees still standing here and there.

Riding around the bunch, the boys began pushing them into the open and down the trail. Suddenly, a loud bellow sounded behind them, and as they turned to look, here came a needle-horned cow, trotting toward them with wild eyes, shaking head, and slobbering at the mouth. When she saw them, she bellowed again, a deep bellow unlike anything a cow would make in normal circumstances.

The boys spurred their mounts into the open and raced ahead of the maddened beast with horses running full out. The cow on their tails, the boys leaned over their horses' necks and urged them onto greater speed. In front of them, a tall burnt tree trunk loomed up, and the boys raced their horses on either side of it. Behind them came a loud crash, and as they turned in their saddles to look, they could see the cow had thought it a man and had run full out into it, breaking her neck.

They pulled up and rode back to see what was left of the cow. She had the rabies and in attacking them in total madness, had seen the stump and tried to gore it at full speed. Knowing the threat of rabies was hanging like a pall across the land then seeing it firsthand sickened and terrified them. They left the cattle to trail on down by themselves and built a big fire, where they burned the carcass of the cow so nothing would eat it and get the rabies. But whatever had bitten her had the rabies, so now they knew they had a fight on their hands to keep a lookout for dogs, cats, and the rest of the wild animals around the area contracting it, and they had to stay alert.

Finding someone to share that life would be the next step in Wade's life. During the years Wade lived on the ranch with his brothers, sisters, parents, and grandparents, there were many ranches in the area that were smaller than theirs. There were two larger ranches that had been established by men from Texas driving their longhorns across the country into Western Montana, where they built to stay. One Texan opted to settle his ranch a little east along the southern slope of the great mountain, and the other west of where the thousand acres owned by Wade's family, the Emmerichs, had been originally homesteaded.

Many ranchers' daughters considered Wade or his brothers to be good catches, and already, one of his brothers, Dan, had married a sweet young woman, Eviana, and was homesteading their own land a few miles from the main ranch. Their three children played in their yard near their cabin, with two dogs and some kittens as playmates. Dan worked his land and had cleared some brush and cedars for a field where the runoff from the mountain could be used as extra water besides the creek flowing nearby. Long hours spent in the field above the cabin, he always came back for lunch to check on his young family and enjoy their company before returning to the work in the afternoon. A spring was nearby the cabin, so Eviana didn't need to walk far for water to use in the home. Corrals were placed to the south and against a small stand of oak for shelter for the animals.

Wade enjoyed the visits he had with his brother and his family whenever he was riding the canyon above Dan's place. Knowing Dan was making a wonderful life for himself gave Wade thoughts of finding someone of his own to share his love for the ranch and to raise their own family together.

Early one evening, Dan came into the ranch, driving his wagon with his wife and children with him. Everyone at the ranch came out into the yard to greet them. Then they saw the fear in the eyes of Eviana and tears on the face of the little ones. "What's going on?" asked Henry as he hurried to help the little family out of the wagon.

"Oh, Father," answered Dan, "a rabid coyote came into the yard at the cabin, and when Eviana heard a noise at the door, there he was, looking in at her, slobber from his mouth running down both sides of his face, and he began growling viciously. My darling here ran, grabbed the gun, and shot him through the screen door. The kids were behind the house playing in the shade. Oh my god, Father, what would have happened to them had that mad creature come from their direction instead of the south?" and at that, Ben began to shake.

Henry gathered Eviana into his arms and gave her a gentle hug. "But he didn't, and my brave daughter-in-law did what she had to do in the face of terror. I am so proud of you, my dear."

Eviana hugged him back and said, "Father Henry, I did what I had to do, but that doesn't make it any easier. Never have I seen a more awful sight than that maddened animal. When will it end?"

At that, Mary took her in her arms and after sharing a hug, said, "Oh, Eviana, we all have to live in this rough land, and we will surely overcome the trials and experiences that come to us whether we want them or not. You are a true treasure for our Dan and our grandchildren, and you and they will all survive these things with the help of Father God and your own courage."

■•■

CHAPTER 24

Often in the little town of Indian Flats where he had gone to school years earlier, dances were held, and he and his siblings rode over the range to attend. Dancing was a treasured activity to break up the monotony of an early fall and to get through winter, and when the Emmerich family could get through the snow to a dance, they all went.

One lovely girl from a local family in Indian Flats seemed to set her cap for Wade, and he found her company entertaining and very enjoyable. They talked for hours at picnics and danced together at the dances. Wade began thinking she was the one and felt he was falling in love. She visited the Emmerich ranch with friends and told him she loved it. They began to talk about marriage, and Wade felt happiness beyond measure.

Then a dance was coming up, and he prepared for it, dressing in new jeans, shirt, high-heeled boots with spurs, and batwing chaps made from angora sheep hide with the wool on. Completing his outfit was his high-crowned Stetson. Handsome and dashing to many, he arrived at the dance with expectations of making the announcement of their engagement.

Emmaline Johnson met him outside the long log structure the town used for their combination meeting hall and dance hall. She whispered, "Wade, we can't make any announcement tonight. My parents know I am in love with you and have forbidden me to even dance with you unless you commit to make the conversion to our Mormon religion." Tears dropping from her eyes, she cried brokenly to him she would have to agree with their wishes.

Wade was stunned into speechlessness. He didn't know anything about the religion, except that it had practiced polygamy, and he was dead set against that. He also knew in his heart that there was a God, and he also believed in Jesus Christ being the Son of God, having been raised with his mother reading aloud from the Bible to her children every night. He had read the Book of Mormon, which was the book of this Mormon religion, and thought it a book of many wars and much fighting. Beyond that, he hadn't given it much thought. But to have someone, anyone, tell him he had to join it or else was the wrong thing to do, and he pulled back hard.

Holding Emmaline in his arms as she sobbed, he felt his heart break and told her, "I am a Christian as much as anyone, and although not a member of your faith, your parents have no right to force me to join your church. They don't know me and apparently have no interest in ever knowing me because I will never join any church for those reasons."

Emmaline, shaking with grief, then asked him if he would do it for her. Gently placing Emmaline away from him, he said, "As much as you say you love me and yet ask me to do something like that? Joining the church for those reasons are against everything I stand for. To ask someone to join for those reasons is wrong in every way, and I will never do it." Wade then turned and headed for his horse. Tightening the cinch, he swung onto the horse and rode away from the narrow, twisted thinking of those who thought they could control their daughters and his life.

This incident reminded him of an earlier time when he had ridden across the miles to a dance and had been looking forward to the fun to be had there after a long summer of cutting and hauling hay. He had asked a comely young woman to dance, and as they got onto the floor, her mother came marching across the room and grabbed her daughter by the arm. "You will not dance with a gentile!" was the comment as she dragged her embarrassed daughter from the dance floor, and his embarrassment was as bad as the girl's. He had walked out of that dance and rode half the night to get back to the ranch, where he grabbed the dictionary and looked up the definition for *gentile* because the way the mother used the word, it sounded like a swear word. So at this time, riding to his family and the ranch he loved, he sadly decided he would stay away from the Mormon church as much as possible in the future.

Wade knew he had many friends among the Mormons in Indian Flats and liked and appreciated them. His parents had been baptized members of the Mormon church: his father, Henry, in Holland, where his parents William and Catherine had joined before emigrating; his mother, Catherine, in England, where her parents had joined the church before emigrating. But from the persecution and abuse the Mormons had taken in the east, when they moved into the west, they were defensive and opinionated themselves to a fault against others not of their religion. And Wade felt this effect roll upon himself, and he didn't appreciate it nor like it.

Wade was out in the field setting the canyon water to run across the field in a flood-irrigating method, working up a sweat with his shirt off and muscles flexing as he shoveled and worked with the dry soil. Hearing hoofbeats coming down the trail from Spring Canyon, he paused and leaned on the shovel, watching until the rider appeared. Recognizing a friend from Indian Flats, Davie Clay, Wade called a hello out and walked over to where Davie was tying up his horse. "What brings you across the mountain on such a hot spring day?"

Davie grinned and held out his hand, and as they shook hands, he told Wade, "I thought you'd forget the horse race we are holding on the Fourth of July. You've got to come, Wade, and ride Teacup! We both know how fast he is, and you ought to win some money, and I will, too, because I will bet on you!"

Wade didn't have to think very long to give Davie his answer because he loved a good horse race and knew his little mustang Teacup could win everything. He had named him Quarter Teacup So because he could turn on a quarter, and he was so smooth riding, Wade had once won money on a bet he could run him across a flat carrying a cup of tea and not spill it. He did it and won the bet.

"Come on down to the house, and we'll have a cup of coffee, Davie, and you can have some of Mother's fresh baked cinnamon rolls. We'll make a plan!"

On the men's arrival at the house, Davie caused considerable excitement among Wade's younger sisters, both of whom had a crush on him. Davie was quite backward and talked with a slight lisp, and a pretty girl's attention was almost more than he could handle. Although this was a problem to him, it wasn't a problem to Carrie, who had known him during the years they had gone into Indian Flats to school and was quite taken with him. Libby was too bashful to say much but refused to leave the room and got the cups down before Carrie could, so Carrie grabbed the coffee pot and poured the coffee. Then they both served the cinnamon rolls, complete with napkins. Davie secretly loved the attention but didn't want Wade to know it and knew Wade was watching every interaction with great interest.

As they sat at the table with Wade's sisters, not a lot of horse racing discussion took place, but interest and questions about the dance the night of the fourth took up the conversation. Davie was usually the *caller* at the square dances and did a great job. Carrie asked, "Are you going to be too busy calling the dances to dance?"

Face turning red, Davie said, "I am going to make sure I'm not."

Libby stated shyly, "I think it only fair you save me from being a wallflower. I hope you won't forget I am going to be at the dance too."

Looking desperately to Wade for escape and seeing nothing in his face but amusement, Davie suggested he get going for the long ride home. Then working up his courage, he looked at both girls and said, "I think you better be there for the Fourth of July festivities. When I wear out, there will be plenty of others to dance with." By this time the red hit his ears, and he went through the door like he was smothering.

Wade raised his eyebrows at his sisters, grinned at Libby, who pulled a face at him, and followed Davie. Outside, after Wade teased Davie about his admiration society, they made plans for the race. Waving goodbye, Davie rode back up the trail into Spring Canyon on his way back across the mountain. Wade saw Davie at the fourth celebration, and Davie told him, "My trail was smoking all the way home. I was so hot from all your sisters' attentions!"

CHAPTER 25

Life delivered another turn he hadn't planned on. One day, a rider came out from town, carrying a packet of mail. One of the letters was addressed to Wade, serving notice he was to serve his country across the ocean in France where the First Great War was raging.

Walking alone in the cedars, holding the letter from the War Department, trying to get his breath between gulps of sobs catching in his throat, he fell to the ground and clutched the dry desert granite soil, hanging onto it as though it and it alone could save him. He didn't know how he could ever leave his beloved family and ranch, and who would take care of his carefully grown herd of Herefords? Would he ever come home, or would a German bullet end his life on foreign soil? So many questions, and the scream of "No" rang in his brain.

He had been raised to treasure his birthright in America since his parents had been emigrants and had to apply for citizenship and finally gotten it. Sacrificing all they had in Holland, they had renounced their Dutch heritage and sought citizenship in America. As they raised their American-born children in the west, they taught them the value of a free land and the right to worship their God as they pleased. Wade understood the value of his American-born heritage and realized this was his time to stand up for the freedoms his parents had sacrificed so much for and defend the nation even with his life if that is what it took.

He pulled himself to his feet and brushed off the dirt and then fell into a cedar and clutching the boughs in his face, he breathed their scent and prayed he would come home to embrace that precious smell again. He pulled handfuls of sage leaves and crushed them in his hands, smelling the luscious sweet scent and again praying for strength to be a man unafraid about this and determining he would be coming home when his time in the service was up.

That night, Wade had a dream that a plane landed in the front yard, and a man with a tall striped hat got out and pointed at him and said, "You will go to war, young man!"

From the War Department letter, instructions informed him of dates, places, and the time he would leave. Telling his family was no easy task. His mother grasped her apron and crying, left the house and went for a long walk. Praying, no doubt, in secret and solitude for his protection and well-being. She and her husband were baptized Mormons but not practicing because of distance from town and church. His dad, with tears welling up in his eyes, grasped Wade's hands and then hugged him hard, telling him how proud he was of him and that he felt deeply that he would return with honor. His sisters and brothers all were shook to the core yet supported and encouraged him.

One younger brother said he was joining the army and would be over there with him. In those days only one or two sons were allowed into the war because of the need of family at home and the brother just younger was deferred because of that. According to the War Department letter, he would report for duty later that fall but wouldn't leave the American continent.

After seemingly a very short time, Wade was headed for Fort Wayne in the city where his parents had arrived a few years before from their native land as emigrants. Upon arrival, Wade was sent to the infirmary, where he received his clothing, which consisted of an army tan woolen uniform, belt, underwear, tall lace-up boots that came to his knees, and a Stetson hat with wide, round brim and a crease in the crown. He also received a compass with US stamped onto it and a US pocket watch. A small Bible that fit into his pocket and a small book of rules and regulations for soldiers completed the things he received.

Shortly after basic training where Wade learned hand-to-hand combat and won all the footraces and could outshoot all the recruits, he found himself on a train across the country to New York. Upon arrival there, the soldiers were herded like so many cattle onto a ship that set sail that day. One young man came up to him and announced they would be bunkmates. Holding out his hand, he introduced himself to Wade as Lane Cook from Chicago. He said, "I haven't been out of Chicago in my life, and now I am supposed to go halfway across the world. Hell, Wade, I hope I come back. If you watch my back, I'll watch yours."

Wade grinned at him and said, "Well, the letter I received said I wouldn't leave American soil. Here we are, and we're leaving American soil! We have to put our faith in our Lord and plan on not drowning crossing the great water!"

In the ocean crossing, Wade discovered he hated the endless waterscape, and since he couldn't swim, he received a lot of hazing from fellow soldiers for a "dirt farmer to be on this much water." Although he didn't get seasick, he hated the big waves and constant rocking of the ship. He couldn't wait to get on land, where the earth wasn't moving.

When the ship reached foreign soil and they all disembarked, Wade and his friend Lane kept together. They all were issued gas masks and had training in their use, an ugly and awkward contraption that hung around the neck but a necessity for life. Assignments to companies were received, and both Wade and Lane were assigned the 111th Division Company A.

Warnings from officers about night duty responsibility included orders to shoot anyone in the area with no orders to be there. Wade was called to attention, and his commanding officer stopped in front of him. "Soldier, you are hereby selected to be a runner between the front lines and rear guard. Also, you will be a sharpshooter."

Wade thought of his ability to run and shoot. He wondered what was facing him and how he had placed himself in this position because he could outrun and outshoot everyone.

One night, Wade drew night duty and was on patrol. A sound from the brush and trees nearby had him cocking his weapon and preparing to fire, yet just before he sprayed the area with his machine gun, he shouted, "Who goes there?"

His officer called back it was he and pray God to not shoot! Unbeknownst to Wade, his commanding officer had taken sick and had rushed into the brush with diarrhea. Had Wade followed orders, he would have killed him. His commander asked him why he hadn't shot first and asked questions later. Wade replied that he never shot at sound until he identified it first. They agreed this incident never happened, then his commanding officer told him he could have been court-martialed because of this.

CHAPTER 26

Having free time one mail day, he took his letter from home and walked up a tall ridge lined with pines and sat beneath a pine to read it. He became so homesick, he wrote an answer that he prayed daily for his parents, grandparents, brothers, and sisters and that they would all stay well and be there when he got home. And how were the cattle? Did the range look okay, and were they getting any rain? That it rained there often and sometimes they were miserable with it.

He couldn't write anything about the war, or the letter would be censored. He couldn't tell his family that during a terrible fight in the Argonne Forest in France, the enemy were firing incessantly, and he was selected as a runner from the officers directing the action to the front with messages. The snipers in the trees were all after him, and he could hear the bullets whine as they flew by his head as he ran, twisting and turning like a rabbit being chased by coyotes.

Once he heard the dreaded sound of an incoming shell from a cannon, and he dove into a wash as it went overhead, landing and blowing a monster pine tree away, leaving a gaping hole a few yards ahead of him. Wade sat there among the pines and thought of the fighting in the trenches he had done. On a particularly muddy ridge, the enemy began firing upon him and his company. He and Lane found themselves shoulder to shoulder digging a trench deep enough to give them somewhat of a cover.

As they got into the trench, he heard a splat and looking sideways, saw Lane fallen over backward with a bullet between his eyes. He took his rifle and emptied it into the trees ahead, where someone screamed, then he heard someone falling through the branches of a tree. Jumping from the trench, he ran up to where the enemy soldier lay and taking his bayonet, stabbed it into the body until he became sick and vomited until he couldn't stand up.

Walking back to where Lane lay, he turned him into the partly dug trench and placed his helmet upon his chest, making sure his hands were on his chest. Then he dug with his bayonet into the bank until it collapsed, partially covering Lane's body. Praying for his soul and for peace for his spirit, Wade knelt and cried for his friend. Vowing to contact his family personally after the war, Wade felt in Lane's pockets until he found his little Bible and US pocket watch, which he placed in his own pocket. He took Lane's hand and told him he would personally give these items to his family when he found them after the war. Sitting there in the muddy partially dug trench by his friend's body, Wade cried until he felt he would pass out. Finally standing, he kept digging dirt until the sides of the trench covered Lane's body.

Some of the trenches were deep since many men had dug into them for protection, and one was partly full of muddy water from rains. When Wade jumped into it, he slipped and fell on a mound. Beneath his hands, he discovered the mound to be a dead body covered in slime and mud, and it stunk with the horrible smell of death when uncovered. Wade didn't think he would ever be able to get that stink and feel off his hands and clothes. Out of the trench, the rain helped somewhat to wash mud from his clothes but chilled him to the bone at night. Sometimes he felt he would never warm up again.

Sickness was prevalent throughout the unit, and Wade had himself a terrible cold that he never thought he would get over. The icy rain and water knee deep in the trenches constantly wore at the soldiers, and some died at their sickest. Keeping in the trenches saved them from bullets and some cannon shells, but Wade wondered if disease would wipe them all out.

✦

CHAPTER 27

He did tell his family about walking with some soldiers down the street in a town. Some girls began yelling from a balcony to them, leaning over and laughing and pointing. Wade decided it wouldn't hurt to climb the grapevine up the railing to where he could visit with them until they finally made him realize they were trying to tell him in French that the police were coming. In that French town, the police were not German but didn't want any soldiers causing mischief with the locals.

In his letter, he asked his sister to send him some sagebrush because he missed it so. "Oh, dear Eliza, how I wish I could be home with you and the rest of the family. I miss the mountains, sunsets, cattle, and even the endless sagebrush flats. The smell of the sage after a rain is from heaven. There is no smell like it over here. Although the pines are beautiful, there is pain and horror here, and beauty fades quickly when we are knee deep in mud, which never leaves our clothes."

In a reply letter some months later when the mail caught up with him, there was a packet of sagebrush. Wade carried that packet inside his shirt pocket until he arrived home, and by that time, little remained of it but its scent, and that was always sweet and fresh. His nickname in the service from that day on became Old Sagebrush!

When Wade and his unit were sent into the forest of Verdun, he thought at least here were trees and rocks and a mountainous area. Maybe his life in the mountains would give him as edge. As he crawled around the base of a tall pine, he noticed a flash of a rifle barrel high in a tree ahead of his unit. Knowing it was a sniper, he took careful aim and pulled the trigger. Screaming, an enemy soldier fell from the tree, clutching his stomach. When he fell, he kept screaming. Wade lay there and watched for other enemy soldiers. None appeared. Evidently, the sniper was alone and had been well hidden.

He got to his knees and then carefully to his feet. Looking around the tree trunk, he could still hear moans coming from the soldier. Walking through the underbrush and trees, Wade came upon the wounded man. Standing there, staring down at the man he knew would die very soon, Wade got no satisfaction, just sickness from having to kill to save his own life and the life of his fellow unit. Thankfully, the fellow died as he watched him. Not wanting to finish him off with another bullet, Wade had debated leaving him to die slowly but knew he needed to finish him. Glad he was done, Wade walked away.

Shortly, finding another terrible battle raging ahead of them, their commanding officers called them together and crouching beneath a low gully, informed them of intent to capture a certain ridge leading up to a crucial town they were trying to protect from the Germans. They were told every weapon of war imaginable was being launched at them from that armament below and that they may not survive but to stick together and try to get through.

As the firing became intense and bullets were dropping his infantry unit around him, Wade held his weapon at waist level, bayonet extended on the barrel of the rifle, and with the determination and courage of a soldier in battle, he fought and ran and dodged until he could see the top of the hill. He knew he had killed some of the enemy, but he also knew many of his fellow infantry had died in this bloody battle for the top. When the few soldiers remaining reached the top with Wade, they discovered from 128 in their unit, there were eighteen left, and none of their commanding officers were left standing. This battle left them walking wounded in body and soul, and this was something Wade never mentally or physically recovered from. For the rest of his life, if a loud sound was made behind him, he would jump and yell. Just couldn't help it.

After winning that battle, there seemed to be endless others and new soldiers to replace those lost. He couldn't tell his family any of these things, yet to receive letters from home whenever or wherever they caught up with him, and soak up a bit of normalization in a war of horror-filled days helped keep him sane.

Then one day, Commanding Officer Colonel Luftwick was by his side in a battle to secure a bridge. Keeping it from being blown up were the orders, and they had fought frantically through a day and a half, with the enemy shooting continuously with canons, trying to blow it up. Suddenly, a scream ripped the air, and a soldier next to Wade was choking and gagging in an effort to get air. Wade's commander shouted to get the gas masks on. After tearing the apparatus loose and placing it on his head, Wade discovered there was no air coming through. He began smothering and tore it off, gasping in yellow nerve gas that the Germans had exploded to fill the air. Colonel Luftwick jerked his mask off and placed it on Wade, screaming at him to breathe, then he put it back on and gasped the air until Wade needed it again, all along walking him to the back trenches where the medics were.

When they got there, Wade was more dead than alive, and the doctors worked to restore his oxygen level before loading him into a van for transport to a hospital in France. Spending months in the hospital, he was in a black void from which he felt he would never return, fighting for every breath he took. One day in the hospital room shared with sixteen other soldiers, Wade felt his lungs shutting down completely. He shuddered and fought and during his struggles to breathe, fell out of the bed and hit the floor.

As the nurse came running, she called for the doctor, and they grabbed him and held a mask to his face. The fall had jolted his lungs and somehow caused a lot of the infection in his lungs to give way, and he began to cough and vomit. Getting rid of the blockage helped some, and from the oxygen administered by the doctor, Wade felt air moving into his lungs with every breath. And from that moment on, he began to mend. Later on, he told his family that in his death throes, he regained his life.

Finally, he grew well enough to walk around a bit. Wade begged to be released to go back to his troop. The doctors were hesitant but finally allowed him to leave. He headed for the train station, where he boarded a train headed for the front lines. At a stop, Wade became disoriented and got off the train. Staggering along, he was grabbed from behind. Two Military Police had him in tow, one stating, "Come on, soldier, you trying to desert? What are you, drunk? You're going to the lockup!" Wade didn't know what was happening as his body was beginning to shut down again. When the MPs got him to their headquarters, an officer stepped out of a nearby door. Grabbing Wade by the shoulder, he stared at him, then the MPs. "This boy was wounded at the front, and now he is sick again. If anything happens to him, I'll see you both court-martialed."

Wade looked up and into the concerned eyes of his commanding officer Colonel Luftwick, who had shared his gas mask with him when his had plugged and saved his life.

Wade was taken back to the hospital where he was declared sick with pneumonia, where he stayed until the end of the Great War. Eventually, Wade's natural good health and strong body helped the medicines heal him to return from the abyss, from where he nearly lost his life.

The doctors and nurses were superb. One nurse came in and wrote a letter home for him, and this reached his family months after he actually had arrived home. The mail service during wartime was interrupted and almost nonexistent. This left a terrible hole in family life on American soil. No letters from him in months, and then letters from his parents and sisters and brothers began returning, stamped "MIA" and "UNKNOWN." Their grief knew no limit, and yet his dear mother kept writing, telling him all the news she could think of, as if she had just heard from him. Keeping everything going at home and not allowing the thought that he was dead into any of their minds took all her strength and determination.

— • —

CHAPTER 28

Mary was a strong, kind woman, possessing many pioneer skills needed for their way of life. While Wade was gone, she continued raising her younger children and guiding and encouraging her older ones. She was the ballast to the family during these difficult years.

She learned how to doctor her own family and helped her sister-in-law on a neighboring ranch when she gave birth. Mary became friends with a band of Indians living nearby, and learned from them herbs and plants that helped with healing various sicknesses.

One day, a little Indian boy rode into the yard and sat his pony. Not getting off alerted the family something was wrong. The little guy just sat there and stared at the house. Mary walked outside and spoke to him. Then she discovered he had a stick going into his cheek and appeared to come out in his mouth. She called to Henry to come help him off the horse and carry him inside. She reassured the child and laid him down on one of the beds. Then with dexterity, she expertly cut the stick off on the outside of the cheek then pulled it on through the hole and into and out of his mouth.

It bled hard for a moment, and she kept calm and laid a poultice of quaking aspen bark inside and outside the wound. Keeping the child calm was her main concern until she could get the cheek partially numb from an aspen tree bark poultice, then she quickly and carefully stitched it shut. When she was through, she gave the little boy another poultice of warm mash made from service berry and milkweed. Pressed against the wound it helped keep swelling down and also helped with fever.

After a few hours, the boy got up and walked out the door. As he got on his horse, he stopped and looked at Mary and held a hand up then rode out of the yard. Mary went to the table and sat with her head in her hands, wondering if the Indians would retaliate if the boy died from infection.

Several days later, the dogs began barking. Through the gate and into the yard rode a group of Indians, included among them were some squaws and the little boy. They were very solemn, and they dismounted from their horses. Mary walked out with Henry by her side and their children watching from the porch.

One of the men stepped forward with a bundle in his arms. "For you," he signed and gave it to Mary. Then the child she had stitched up and a woman she assumed was his mother came forward. The child smiled at her, and she smiled back. His mother also carried a packet, which she presented to Mary. Then she said in broken English and signing, "You, wyno squaw!"

Mary was puzzled as to what that meant and asked back, "What does that mean?"

The Indian man then replied, "You, good woman!"

Dashing back tears with her hand, Mary tentatively reached out a hand to the Indian child and woman, who both stepped toward her, and she hugged them both.

After offering the group coffee and cake, they ate and smiling, got on their horses and rode back down the wagon road toward the river, where their camp was a few miles away. Mary went to her table and opened the packages the Indian people had given her. Inside one was various plants, dried and ready for use in her doctoring. Inside the packet on a piece of buckskin was drawn various pictures of people in degrees of illness, including broken bones, and a drawing of which herb and plant to use. In the other packet was dried venison and dried plants to use as tea.

What a wonderful day for Mary with relief that she had made new friends among the Indians and learned about more methods to help doctor the sick. She became known all across the mountains as the wyno squaw, and she felt very proud of the title. During times of unrest among the Indians and settlers, the Emmerich family was protected and never bothered even by the troublemakers among the Indians.

Wade's brother Ben met a woman in her thirties who showed a deep and determined interest in him and wrote him many letters encouraging and enthusiastic. Ben finally asked her to dinner. He rode into a town to the north of Indian Flats that had a railroad spur and then rode the train about seventy miles farther north to the town of Sulphur Springs, where she and her family lived. She had gone to school to be a teacher and was teaching there in her hometown.

Dorrie Mathews was well-known as a talker and schemer and hadn't many dates, and so when Ben crossed her path, she set her cap for the unsuspecting country boy. At dinner that evening, she asked, "Where would you like to spend the rest of your life, Ben, on that ranch or in a town where you could get work and buy a home and raise your family with a school and church for the children?" She kept this line of questions up all evening yet managed to feed his ego with her compliments.

Before Ben knew it, he was trapped hook, line, and sinker. A wedding was being planned, and he began working on a small cabin a short distance from his parents' home. He also took up a homestead where he could prove up on it after he was married. Upon meeting Dorrie, his mother commented to Wade in a letter that she was strong-minded and opinionated and hoped Ben would be happy with such a city girl.

Ben wrote to Wade also and said he sometimes wondered if he had made the right decision that Dorrie was going to live on the ranch with him, not him living in town with her. When Wade read the letter, he grinned to himself about that. His grin was quickly replaced with a frown because he felt strongly there was a dishonesty about Dorrie that would cause trouble in their tight-knit family. He silently prayed that would prove untrue since he and Ben had planned for years to work together with the ranch to build it into something worth having.

Two of Wade's sisters began dating some men who had come to work in the mines that were going strong in the area because of the war and the need for the minerals being produced. One sister married her suitor, who was a fine man and who loved her dearly. Her letters to her brother in France held a note of her love for her new husband. Wade felt that sometimes he was missing all the good things in the world while in that foreign land.

One day, mail call found him with two letters from home—unheard of for him—which brought a joy he felt into his bones. Taking them unopened, he tucked them inside his shirt, and telling the nurse at the hospital he needed to take a walk, he left the hospital and headed for a small hill nearby, upon which grew some pines and shrubbery.

Gasping for breath, out of shape, and still healing from his lung wounds, he clambered up to a small boulder protruding out the dirt. Sitting upon it, he could look below at the activity around the hospital and into the town but still be alone. He dug into his pocket and retrieved one letter, addressed from his mother. She told of the happenings with the little Indian boy and of the friendship of the Emmerichs among the Indians. She told of the garden and how large it was and how many jars of vegetables she and his grandmother had canned. In it, she expressed the hope and prayers for him they all had, that he would soon be home forever with them, never once expressing her terror that they might never know what happened to him and never once telling him his letters had been returned with the ugly black stamp of MIA on them.

Tears filled his eyes, and he knew he would recover and eventually be back on his beloved ranch with his family. Then he pulled the second letter out, addressed from his sister Libby. To his extreme joy, he discovered it contained missives from all of his sisters. Carrie wrote that she wanted him to know that she was in love with a young man who had been working in the town of New Guinea in a mine and had become acquainted with him at a dance. They planned their marriage for the early spring of next year and how she hoped he would return by then.

Then she went on to tell him that his sister Eliza had married a young man by the name of John Maxwell. They had eloped and came back to live in New Guinea, where he worked in a mine near the town. One morning, Eliza walked out of their cabin, and a rattlesnake had struck her leg. She screamed, and a neighbor came running to see what was wrong. She showed him the place near the cabin where the snake was coiled, still buzzing, and then her leg with fang marks.

Old Don grabbed a nearby shovel and killed the snake then grabbed Eliza up and ran with her down into town to the doctor. The doctor couldn't do much, and Eliza died the next day. It was a tragedy for the family and Eliza's husband. At her funeral, John sat as if in a trance, and afterward, as people were visiting around the grave, he walked away and went to their little cabin on the hill above town. When Mary and Henry went after him, they discovered him packing a valise and hitching up a horse to his buggy. Mary hugged him tightly and asked him what on earth he was going to do. He looked at them both and said he couldn't live if he had to see her grave every day. He was leaving, and asked for no one to try to find him. He did leave, and none of the family had heard of him since.

Wade held his head and cried. No one at home was supposed to die. He figured if anyone would, it would be him.

In letter, she told him about wearing her dad's coveralls and riding the old black gelding astride for the first time up in a cedar draw not far from the front gate of the ranch. She and Carrie had taken turns wearing the overalls while they rode the gentle old horse around in the cedar draw. What fun they had! Carrie wrote that he needn't worry his sisters were getting bad. They were the same good girls he had left at home, but they just had to try because it looked so much more fun than riding side-saddle!

She also mentioned Davie Clay had asked her to ride out with him in the nearby canyons several times. Carrie hinted that there just might be a romance budding. Carrie wrote that she had gone to work at a mine that had started up not far from the ranch and had a boardinghouse where she worked doing laundry. She was somewhat of a flirt, and Wade worried about her.

At the end, Libby wrote that she was keeping busy helping her mother and grandmother on the ranch with meals, milking the two cows, and doing family laundry. Always much to do, she loved the ranch as much as Wade did, and she loved the huge garden they had planted. She enjoyed the harvest and helped drive the team for her dad when the boys were busy elsewhere.

After reading the letters, Wade felt uplifted, and in better spirits. The walk down the hill went better than climbing it, and when he entered the hospital, he had a smile for the nurses and his fellow patients. Walking over to one bed where a young man was swathed in bandages across his head and eyes, he pulled up a chair and took his limp hand. He began talking to him, telling him about the ranch and some of the things he had done as a kid. Suddenly, he realized the boy's hand had clasped his, and he felt a strong clasp at that. Although the fellow didn't speak, Wade knew he heard him, and after visiting with him for a while, he returned to his bed area.

Thinking of someone else's pain helped ease his own, and a strong determination came over him that he was going home soon to his beloved ranch in the West and that his lungs would heal.

He also resolved that when he headed home, he would find out where Lane Cook came from and go visit his family. He owed that much to Lane, anyway. Again, an overwhelming feeling of gratitude to God for the protection he had received in battle and that although he had been wounded terribly by the yellow mustard gas, he still lived, facing a bright future, while many of his comrades were still on foreign soil in mouldering graves.

He sat at his desk near his bed and wrote a letter to his commanding officer, asking him to help him be released from the hospital. Realizing this officer could help in finding Lane's family, he also asked for information on the young man and briefly explained the facts behind his request.

In a week's time, Colonel Luftwick was working on papers covering his desk and came upon a letter from Wade Emmerich, addressed from the military hospital in France. Request for his discharge papers along with the approval of Dr. Carrington were the contents of Wade's letter, with a heartfelt thank-you to his commanding officer for saving his life that night near the train station when he had been so ill with pneumonia.

Then Wade's letter shifted to Lane Cook, and as the colonel read further, tears burned behind his eyes, and the colonel sat back in his chair, thinking of all the young men who had fought so loyally and unselfishly for the war effort against Germany, not the least of those for whom German bullets found their mark, leaving broken hearts behind in America and across the world. Some were merely declared MIA, no body found. Calling out to an orderly, he gave him orders to research and find Pvt. Lane Cook's family. The colonel stiffened his back, took up pen and paper, and began the process of honorable discharge for young Mr. Wade Emmerich.

On a day when Wade was sitting beside the bed, talking to Private Collins with the head wound, he heard a feeble whisper from the young man. He leaned closer and heard him say, "Help me sit up."

So Wade reached beneath his shoulders, and as he gently lifted him, he stuck pillows behind his back and neck. Private Collins said, "Now take these bandages off my face and eyes."

"Just hold on a minute, private," said Wade, then he jumped up and almost sprinted into the next room, where he found a nurse assisting another man. He called, "Private Collins is awake and wants the bandages off now."

The nurse burst into smiles as she hurried to join Wade at the private's bedside. Taking his hand, she told him, "This is the best news I have received all week. You must wait for the doctor, and he will be here shortly. Please just be patient a little while longer."

Jerking his hands away, Private Collins reached at the bandages, tearing at his head, as though he was suffocating. Wade reached for him, and as he held him, he talked to him about the day outside being sunny and bright, carrying with it the hope of a beautiful spring and a beautiful recovery. The nurse looked at Wade approvingly and mouthed that she was going for the doctor.

Presently, into the room came a tall man accompanied by the nurse. As he shook Wade's hand, he said, "Glad you are here. He needs a friend right now."

Private Collins said, "Is it that bad? Do I really need someone to hold me up when you tell me I will be blind?"

The doctor grabbed his hand and said, "Not hardly, Collins. You will be just fine. You just need to work on your faith a little." Then the doctor began unwrapping the bandages slowly and carefully and sometimes with the nurse wiping warm water on the cloth to get it to soften enough to pull away from the skin.

Finally, the eyes were exposed, and the doctor said, "Now, Collins, open your eyes slowly."

As the young soldier's eyes opened, he looked at the doctor intently, then at the nurse, and finally at Wade standing nearby. "I can see! Oh my god! Thank you! Thank you!"

Wade, knowing he would be all right, quietly left the bedside and walked back into his room, thinking of the miracles wrought by doctors and nurses on the front lines as well as in the hospitals. Without them, how many more soldiers would never come home?

CHAPTER 29

Three months later, in early summer, a train whistle was heard in Salt Lake City, Utah Territory. As the train idled at the stop, passengers began disembarking. After several ladies had been escorted from the train, a single young man stood in the doorway. Dressed in army fatigues, high-laced boots reaching to his knees, Stetson hat pulled just right, and bag in hand, he finally stepped from the train onto the platform of the station. With his wool uniform buttoned to his throat, he felt the Utah heat hit him like a wave from a furnace. Compared to where he had been, it felt like a bit of heaven touched him.

He walked slowly away from the train station, loving the sight of the mountains covered in grass and thinking of his family yet another journey away, this time by horse back. Saying silent prayers of thanks, he kept his course toward Fort Wayne on the ridge in the distance, red brick buildings glowing in the softly setting sun, where he had begun his journey to the other side of the world.

Approaching the building, he looked for the mustering-out office. Finding it, sitting back beside barracks and other offices, he walked inside. An officer was sitting at a polished desk with paperwork spread out upon it. When the officer looked up, Wade stood at attention, saluted, and stated his name, rank, and serial number. "At ease, soldier. What can I help you with?"

"I have an honorable discharge here, sir, with my commanding officer Colonel Luftwick's signature on it." Carefully placing it on the Staff Sergeant's desk, Wade stepped back a pace and waited while it was scanned by the man.

Looking at Wade, he studied his face. "Why are you here three months after being discharged, private? It didn't take that long to cross the ocean and continent, did it? Not with the modern means of transportation."

Wade said, "I had a stop to make along the way, sir."

"You want to tell me about it?"

Pressing Wade for details that weren't any of his business riled Wade, but he fought his anger down, and briefly explained about Private Cook. When Wade had left the hospital the day Private Collins had his bandages removed and knew he could see, he went for a walk up on the hill above the hospital where he had often gone seeking solitude and quiet to read letters from home or just think. When he got to his favorite spot to sit, he took out the last letter he had received. It was from his dear father, to whom he had been very close all his life. Father Henry hadn't written many letters, but his mother had always included comments from him to his son in her letters, and these, Wade cherished. Now here was his first and only letter from Henry, and Wade was afraid to open it, thinking something had happened to his beloved mother.

It began,

Dear Son,

I write with heavy heart today because I do not know if you are alive to read this. All our letters have been coming home, stamped with a black MIA. UNKNOWN. Your dear mother's heart is breaking but she keeps us all encouraged and determined to not accept that you might be dead.

Please, Son, if you get this, have someone write to us and tell us how you are. We are praying for you every morning and every night and all day long. Your sisters and brothers are worried sick and so are your grandparents. This war has to end soon, and we think it will. Know that we love you, and I am sending this with the great prayer that it will not come back.

Your loving Father, Henry.

Sitting in shock, not realizing that all the months he had lain in the hospital in France, all his mail could not find him. Much of that time, he had been in such a state of delirium, he couldn't know the mail was going astray. No one but himself and his commanding officer knew what had happened to him. Sick at heart, he arose from his rock bench and walked quickly down the hill to the hospital.

Asking a nurse for writing paper and a pen, he immediately wrote a reply and then asked for directions to the telegraph office. The nurse informed him that was too far for him to travel. "I am being released soon, and I demand a conveyance to the telegraph office. If the hospital won't provide one, I will walk if it takes me all week!"

She pointed to the door and said, "Go out and turn to your right. There should be a little stable nearby where the hostler keeps his animals. He should be there, and he can take you wherever you need to go. Just get back as soon as possible."

Getting the hostler to send him to the telegraph station with a boy driver didn't take long, and he was able to send his telegraph.

Mother and Father STOP I am alive STOP I will be arriving in a few months because I will have been Honorably Discharged. STOP Your loving Son, Wade

Unknown to Wade, his commanding officer Colonel Luftwick had already telegrammed his parents, telling them of his hospital sojourn and recent release, including his planned stop to see Private Cook's family. This telegram hadn't reached them before Henry sent his despairing letter.

Looking at the man sitting behind the shiny desk in a position of authority, Wade wondered if he had ever been on a battlefield. No matter, he requested Wade's story, and he would give it to him.

Upon arrival back at the hospital and paying the hostler for the use of the cart and horse, he walked into the hospital. The nurse approached him, smiling, handing him a sheet of paper. Upon it was engraved his discharge papers, and he was finally free to return to his beloved American continent. Taking them in hand, with a hug from the nurse and handshakes all around from the various patients in the ward, he quickly walked to his bunk, where he began packing his few belongs into a bag. As he stood beside the train tracks at the depot where he would catch the train for the coast, he again silently thanked the Supreme Being in Whose hands all lives rested.

After a long, arduous journey across the European continent and upon the waters of the Atlantic Ocean, he at last reached America. As he watched the Statue of Liberty across the bay, he thought of the feelings his grandparents must have had as they had emigrated from Holland years before. He watched carefully for sight of Ellis Island, where they had made it through into their new future. He wondered silently how many lives had been enriched as they transferred onto the free American soil and felt pain in his heart for those turned away. And he said a prayer of thanks to the Lord for his gift of freedom to himself and his parents, brothers, sisters, uncles, aunts, and grandparents. What a journey they had taken to get to freedom. His heart swelled with joy to imagine the ranch and family and the rest of his life in front of him.

Looking at the papers Colonel Luftwick had supplied him at their meeting before he left France, he memorized the address and names of Private Cook's family. Living for years in Chicago after they had received word of their son's death, they had moved into the upper reaches of New York, where the city didn't reach and they had a farm and a few head of livestock. It was into this pastoral setting Wade arrived in the morning of a beautiful early spring day.

Walking from the main road where he had caught a ride with a man going in the general direction of the Cook homestead, Wade looked for the tall farmhouse with the weathercock vane on top.

Around a bend, and there it was. And here came a barking dog, full of himself and making the most of a show of defense of his owners' property. Wade stopped, knelt down on one knee, and spoke softly to the brave little animal. The dog looked puzzled then began wagging his tail. Pretty soon, together with Wade, he walked quietly up to the door, where Wade knocked.

As the door opened, Wade saw blond hair tied up with a green ribbon and a set of intelligent bright-blue eyes in the face of a lovely girl. As she looked at him, he found his tongue and asked if this was the home of Mr. and Mrs. Andrew Cook. "Yes, it is. May I ask who is calling?"

Wade told her his name, and she turned away from the door, asking him to wait there. Presently, a stooped older man came to the door and asked "Mr. Emmerich, I am told. What can I do for you?"

When Wade asked to speak to him and his family for a moment, he hesitated then motioned him inside. After seating Wade, Mr. Cook called for Mrs. Cook and their daughter Lucy.

When they were all seated, Wade began. "Folks, I find this as hard as anything I have ever done. I knew your son Lane in the war. We were friends. The word *friend* is almost sacred to me. A friend has your back in hard times and shares your joy in good ones.

"Lane was happy, determined, honest, and he had integrity. I could count on him with my life, and I was standing right next to him when he died. He had my back up until then, and all I could do was see that he was buried.

"I have brought you his watch and Bible and want you to know he loved each of you with all his heart. He often talked of his sister, Miss Lucy. He wanted you to make the right choices in your life and to choose wisely when it comes to a husband. He told me he wanted his parents to have a good life and not to have to work so hard and hoped he would come home to help you.

"I was told by his commanding officer, Colonel Luftwick, that he had a goodly sum of money saved up, and Colonel Luftwick gave it to me to give to you when I found you. So here it is, folks, and know that I share in your sorrow at the loss of such a fine young man."

Sobbing, Mrs. Cook got up from her chair and came to Wade, who met her halfway across the room. She hugged him tightly and thanked him. Her husband struggled to get up, and Wade grabbed his hand and shook it as the man trembled with emotion. Lucy stood beside the sofa, crying softly. Wade took a bundle from inside his shirt, opened the packet, and handed Mr. Cook Lane's money, a sum of $900, an amazing amount of money to these kind people.

Accepting an invitation for dinner and a room for the night, Wade remained the afternoon and evening, hearing stories about Lane and his life with his family. Wade shared stories from the war with them and found a certain healing deep within his soul after this visit. Morning would find him back on his westward journey following the trails of his grandparents and into his future.

After finishing the narrative, Wade watched the man at the desk. He had leaned back in his chair as Wade had talked and hadn't interrupted. Then sitting up, he nodded toward a chair he hadn't offered Wade before and began stamping and processing the honorable discharge. Calling for an orderly, he instructed him to issue mustering-out pay to Wade.

When Wade received the meager sum, he was dismissed, and as he walked out of the office, he realized he was again a free man: free to come and go as he pleased, free not to have to call anyone sir, free to sleep, free to run, free to walk, free to ride—free to go home to his beloved mountain home!

Looking down the street in Salt Lake City, he realized the lateness of the hour. Walking quickly down a hill into the center of town, he looked for a place to sleep that night. Finding a boardinghouse, he paid for a room for the night and a meal. His stomach told him it was starving and very thirsty. Being told the supper hour would begin in an hour, he took his gear to his assigned room and lay down upon the bed, surprised at the softness and good smell in the room.

ABOUT THE AUTHOR

Patricia grew up on a remote cattle ranch with four older sisters and parents she loved. She was homeschooled on the ranch and taught to ride, rope, drive a team of horses, fix fences, irrigate pastures, and through it all, always remain a lady.

Patsy loved school and reading, so every trip to town found her in the library, checking out boxes of books. After graduation from high school, she studied journalism for a year then met and married her husband, with whom she shared fifty-seven years, raising their three sons.